"You aren't the first to try tricking me into matrimony!"

Tarrant smiled scornfully as he spoke.

Angela bristled; she knew about his reputation with women. "I hope all those women who supposedly want to marry you realize their good fortune in not succeeding!"

She'd planned to stride haughtily away, but caught a heel in the carpet and tumbled across the chair, upending herself.

"Miss Meadows, do you ne

"No! I'm—I'm fine."

Despite her breathless pr

regain her balance. Their eyes met for a brief, appalling second, then she made a beeline for the exit.

"By the way . . . ."

She stopped and faced him. "By the way *what*, Mr. Seaton?"

"It's Tuesday, Miss Meadows, and your panties read Wednesday. If you're going to work for me, you'll need to show more attention to detail."

Angela pinned him with a disgusted stare. "I would rather be a day ahead, Mr. Seaton, than a horse's behind!"

Renee Roszel became a professional writer at the tender age of ten; her hometown newspaper paid her five dollars for a feature article titled ''My Pop Is Tops.'' However, her career didn't really take off until after her two sons started school. She decided to try writing romance novels and hasn't looked back. Renee now combines writing with teaching aerobics and claims that if she could ever learn to control her love of chocolate she'd actually *look* like an aerobics instructor! With apologies to her wonderful husband, she confesses that one of her secret fantasies is to find a ''chocolate magnate'' like Tarrant Seaton—a man who could provide her with chocolate-covered strawberries for the rest of her life.

Renee was recently named the University of Oklahoma's 1991 Writer of the Year.

Books by Renee Roszel

HARLEQUIN TEMPTATION
246—ANOTHER HEAVEN
279—LEGENDARY LOVER
334—VALENTINE'S KNIGHT
378—UNWILLING WIFE

HARLEQUIN AMERICAN ROMANCE
 10—HOSTAGE HEART
129—ANOTHER MAN'S TREASURE

PRINCE OF DELIGHTS

Renee Roszel

Harlequin Books

TORONTO • NEW YORK • LONDON
AMSTERDAM • PARIS • SYDNEY • HAMBURG
STOCKHOLM • ATHENS • TOKYO • MILAN
MADRID • WARSAW • BUDAPEST • AUCKLAND

To Eva Hunter Parrack,
for all the little things over the years

ISBN 0-373-03198-X

Harlequin Romance first edition May 1992

PRINCE OF DELIGHTS

CHAPTER ONE

ANGELA DROPPED her salad fork with a resounding clank, drawing curious glances from the elegantly clad diners at nearby tables. Feeling heat creep up her face, she whispered, "I hope you didn't say what I think you said, Mother."

Minny Meadows dabbed delicately at her pursed lips. "Of course I did, sweetie." She leaned across the fine English bone china and repeated her upsetting revelation. "I said, I had one of my dreams, and it was about you."

Angela stifled a groan, forgetting the expensive lunch she'd been picking at—and the fact that she was picking at it in the poshest restaurant in Seatonville, a restaurant she could ill afford. She clamped her hands together in her lap and swallowed nervously. "About—" she cleared her throat "—me?"

Minny's brown eyes twinkled merrily. "That's why we're here."

Angela's apprehension became mixed with bewilderment. "Here?" She looked around the richly appointed restaurant, candlelit even at midday. "In The Plethora? I thought it was to celebrate my getting the Delila's Delights remodeling contract."

Her mother cast her gaze left, then right, as though she had a great secret to disclose and feared being overheard. "No." She smiled knowingly. "That was just my excuse for coaxing you into this place."

Angela looked at her watch. She didn't have time for riddles. She was worried about leaving her young assistant in charge of her fledgling store, but Minny had insisted they have this lunch. They were celebrating the fact that Delila Seaton herself had hired Angela to help reorganize both the Seaton mansion and the Delila's Delights chocolate factory—or so Angela had thought.

Angela had been aghast when she'd settled into a velvet Queen Anne chair and discovered that the least expensive thing on The Plethora's menu was the fifteen-dollar house salad. She'd hoped, for that price, the house salad included a kitchen sink!

And now her mother was saying they were at this exclusive restaurant because she'd had one of her crazy dreams? Angela had to stop herself from leaping across the table and throttling her. They didn't have an extra thirty dollars plus tax and tip to spend on lemon-sloshed lettuce, and Angela didn't have any desire to dawdle in an opulent restaurant surrounded by silks and diamonds. She looked down at herself. She was clad in a green-and-black-checked synthetic shirtwaist, topped off by a black cardigan. And her mother, forever draped in one wildly tie-dyed jumpsuit or another, appeared more like a fortune-teller than a cutting-edge businesswoman. That was probably because she *was* a self-proclaimed fortune-teller.

Angela took a deep breath, attempting to calm her nerves and steel herself for what was to come. "All right, Mother, if dragging me here wasn't to celebrate getting the Delila's Delights account, then why—?"

"Shh!" Minny cautioned, her expression becoming intent as her eyes darted to the restaurant entrance. "What time is it?"

"It's noon," Angela replied without looking at her watch again. "Mother, I really should be going...."

"Exactly?"

"What?"

Minny glanced back at her daughter. "Is it exactly noon?"

Angela checked the time with a sigh. "Well, as exact as a twelve-dollar watch will get it. I could call the radio station for the time and temperature if—"

"Just let me know when it's one minute after noon," her mother cut in, her eyes shifting back to the gilded door.

Angela rested her elbow on the table and stared down at her watch, observing the second hand travel across its face. She knew better than to argue with her mother when she got into one of her moods. "Okay, ten—nine—eight—"

Minny wagged her hand. "That's good enough, sweetie. Now just keep your eyes on the door."

"Why?"

Minny, never moving her gaze from the ornate entry and never missing a beat, explained matter-of-factly, "Because, Angela, the man who walks through that door at exactly one minute after noon will be your husband."

"My *husband!*" Angela repeated, incredulous.

"There he is!" Minny cried happily. Her voice was low, but to Angela's ears, it sounded as though it had boomed from a loudspeaker. She gaped at her mother, who'd obviously gone off her trolley. Then, as voices around her quieted and heads turned, she realized that her mother was not the only person in the room staring at the man in the doorway. As her pulse raced with irritation and frustration, Angela turned, too. At first she could only see a very tall, very broad silhouette framed in the door. An instant later, the silhouette became the well-dressed form of a man quite familiar to citizens of Seatonville—and Kansas—not to mention single women all over America who would not otherwise have known where Kansas was.

Tarrant Seaton stood there, his smile flashing in the dimness as he spoke to the attentive maitre d'. Dashing Tarrant Seaton—known on society pages as the Prince of Delights, for reasons that had entirely too little to do with his chocolate factories—was the great-grandson of Seatonville's founder, as well as the most sought-after eligible bachelor in a five-state area. His darkly handsome features constantly graced not only Kansas papers, but those of both coasts. A bit belatedly Angela noticed that a dazzling blonde was clinging to his arm.

Tarrant Seaton had just returned from California where he'd opened another Delila's Delights factory. Angela knew that, because his secretary had scheduled Angela for an appointment with him tomorrow so she could become acquainted with the factory's storage areas and begin planning how to modernize them. But considering the excited buzzing in the room, it was obvious that his return had not been general knowledge. However, one lovely woman had evidently been privy to the news.

"Why, he's just as handsome as can be, sweetie. He'll be a perfect husband for you."

Angela shot her mother an unbelieving look. "For heaven's sake, Mother, don't you know who that is?"

"Of course I know. I read the newspapers."

"Well then, isn't it obvious you're mistaken? I mean *me* marry Tarrant Seaton? That's as foolish an idea as ... as me getting picked to be Miss America!"

Minny was clearly surprised. "Are *you* Miss America, sweetie? Why that's simply wonderful! I don't know how I let that slip my mind."

"Oh, Mother," Angela sighed. "I didn't mean... What I mean is, I'm *not* Miss America. I'll *never* be Miss America, and I'll certainly never be Mrs. Tarrant Seaton. Be reasonable." With a sad shake of her head, she added,

"Please, just finish your salad. I have to get back to the store. Richard is competent, but he can't handle—"

"Miss Meadows?"

At the sound of her name, Angela turned to see their tuxedo-clad waiter standing stiffly beside them. "Yes?"

"You have a phone call, Miss Meadows. You may take it in the antechamber."

Angela thanked the dour-faced man, then grimaced at her mother. "See? That's Richard. I told him to call if he had a problem. Could you hurry and eat so we can get out of here?"

Her mother, preoccupied with watching Tarrant Seaton and his female companion being led to a table, waved her away. "Of course, of course. Take your call. I'll be finished in a flash."

Five minutes later, after one more crisis had been averted at her store, which specialized in wire, plastic and wooden storage-space organizers, Angela returned to her table to discover that her mother was missing. Assuming Minny had made a trip to the ladies' room, Angela took her seat and began rummaging in her purse for her wallet, hoping she had enough cash to pay the bill.

"It's all set, sweetie. I told him, and he was happy to hear about it."

"That's nice, Mother. Fifteen percent of thirty dollars plus tax—" Angela looked up from counting her change, blinking in confusion. "What did you say? Who was happy about what?"

Minny seated herself gracefully, spreading her bright blue-and-red tie-dyed sash over the chair's arm like a queen tossing flower petals to her subjects. "Tarrant Seaton, naturally. Why do you think we're here? I told him you two are going to be married. He seemed a bit surprised. What a gentleman he is. Of course, I apologized to the pretty blonde, since she doesn't have a chance with him, now. She's Eden Something. Seems nice . . .''

Angela's eyes had widened in horror as she listened, the extent of her mother's scandalous behavior slowly creeping into her brain. She cast an afflicted glance at Tarrant Seaton and . . . and the Eden person. They were staring at her and her mother. Could she blame them?

"Mother," she whispered raggedly. "You didn't!" She couldn't seem to stop looking at the man who was watching her, his dark gaze holding her captive with an expression that was uncomfortably intent, something between mild curiosity and outright disdain.

A dark brow arched as his eyes traveled from her sale-rack pumps to her home-permed hair. Feeling suddenly defensive, she twisted a raven curl around her index finger. She wanted to shout out that her hair was perfectly fine. Not many people could cut and perm their own hair with even half her success. But she could only stare back, appalled at being sized up like one of her father's not-so-prize hogs at the bankruptcy auction.

Angela chewed the inside of her cheek, transfixed, as his lips twisted in a slow scornful smile. Suddenly cutting her free from his visual grip, he turned to his attractive companion and said something to her. Whatever remark he'd made, it was no doubt at Angela's expense, for the blond woman giggled. They both regarded Angela with one last amused glance before focusing their attention on their menus.

Angela felt at first hot and then clammy as the blood drained from her face. How humiliating! Tarrant Seaton thought she and her mother were crazy, or worse, not worth taking seriously.

"Mother," Angela breathed, "let's get out of here."

"But I'm not finished with—"

"I'll fix you a bologna sandwich at the apartment."
Tossing her money on the table, she hastened toward the
exit, her body stiff with indignation. Thank heaven she
could hear the rustle of her mother's jumpsuit behind her,
because she would rather eat live frogs than look to see if
Minny was following.

"But, Angela, sweetie," her mother called loudly,
turning curious heads, "I thought you might want to meet
Tarrant on our way out."

"I don't think so, Mother," came her harsh whisper.
"I've met just about all of Mr. Seaton I care to meet!"

"What about tomorrow?" Minny asked, sounding
winded as she finally caught up with her daughter at the
door.

Angela halted, feeling as though she'd just stepped on a
Kansas cow patty. "Tomorrow," she repeated dolefully.
"I have that appointment with him, don't I?"

Her mother nodded, smiling happily. "Convenient, isn't
it? You can really get to know each other."

"Oh, jeez..." Pulling open the door, Angela hurried
down the steps to the street exit. "Maybe it was too dark.
Maybe he didn't get a good look at me," she murmured,
hope stirring within her.

"Maybe he'll forget your name, too," Minny offered
helpfully. "But I don't think so. He seems quite smart, and
he said it several times."

Angela spun to face her mother. "You told him my
name?"

Minny shrugged, squinting up in the brightness of this
brisk, first day of April. "Well, I thought a groom ought
to know his bride's name."

"Oh, fine!" Angela turned on her heel, walking toward her shop with their small apartment above it.
"Mother, has anyone ever told you that you can be a—"

She bit her lip. Angry words wouldn't help. The damage was done.

"Be a what, sweetie?"

Angela shook her head. "Never mind."

Obviously undaunted by her daughter's forlorn mood, Minny asked, "What do you think you'll wear to your meeting with Tarrant tomorrow? You want to make a good first impression."

"Good first impression," Angela muttered, her tone despairing. "Why don't I just go to his office wearing a wedding gown, trailing six bridesmaids?"

Minny looked thoughtful for a moment. "I don't know. That doesn't seem like enough bridesmaids for a Seaton wedding."

"Silly me," Angela retorted. "I'm sure that grin he passed me indicated he'd prefer at least twelve bridesmaids."

"He grinned?" Minny's smile broadened. "That's nice."

"Oh, yes, Mother. It was quite a meaningful grin, too. I'm sure it meant he's absolutely delirious with the idea of marriage to me."

Her sarcasm was apparently lost on Minny, who clasped her hands in delight. "It's just as I dreamed. Mind you, I didn't know *who* it was then. Aren't things working out wonderfully?"

Angela chewed the inside of her cheek in irritation. "Mother." She turned toward the shorter woman and placed both hands on her narrow shoulders. "Try to return briefly to the real world. Tarrant Seaton will not only *not* marry me, but he'll fire me the instant I walk into his office. So I wouldn't pick out a silver pattern, if I were you."

Minny shook her head at her doubting daughter. "Angela, will you never learn? I *dreamed* it!"

Realizing she wasn't going to get anywhere with logic—or reminding her mother that frequently her so-called prophetic dreams caused them more trouble than anything else—she absently patted her mother's cheek. "Right. My mistake."

They were standing in front of her shop—Inner Space: Maximum Efficiency for Minimum Areas. Her dreams, her hopes, her whole future depended on the success of her store. She sold individual wire and wooden shelving, drawers, cupboards, countertops, cubbyhole groupings and plastic storage containers, all of which could be stacked or fastened together into space-saving organizers. Plus, she offered a custom consultation service for upgrading and streamlining storage areas and closets for homes and businesses. She was working and living on a shoestring. And then, last week, Delila Seaton, the town's beloved matriarch, had called. That had been Angela's big break—a commission to do a custom revamping of the storage space in both her Seatonville chocolate factory and her mansion. Angela's dreams finally seemed to be coming true.

But now... Angela sighed. There was little left to say. And tomorrow Tarrant Seaton would also have little to say. "You're fired!" wouldn't take long.

"What are you thinking, sweetie? You look a little pale."

Angela felt hysterical laughter bubble up in her throat. She'd just lost an account that would have given them a solid economic foothold—something she and her family had rarely experienced—as well as a good chance for her new business to become a success. But thanks to Minny's eccentricity, that chance was gone. Choosing not to belabor a point that would be lost on her flighty mother anyway, she merely shook her head and entered the colorful container store.

The front wall was taken up with a decorative window display. The other three walls had each been painted a different primary color: red, blue and yellow. The wire containers, which came in those three colors, were arranged on the wall of their respective color. Along two center aisles were less expensive plastic containers of all shapes and sizes. A door near the back led to the custom department where the more expensive wooden modules were exhibited and where she kept a selection of additional catalogs.

Minny glided through the aisles of plastic containers toward the back of the shop. When she reached the stairs that led to their tiny apartment, a sudden thought struck Angela. "Mom, do you realize this is April Fools' Day?"

Her mother turned. "Well, of course I do. What do you take me for? A nitwit?"

This time, Angela didn't bother to stifle her laughter. Tears came to her eyes and she laughed so hard she came down with the worst case of hiccups she'd ever had. Perfectly fitting, Angela decided, considering the rest of her day.

ANGELA RECROSSED HER LEGS and tugged nervously at the hem of her pleated navy skirt. She was fuming. Tarrant Seaton had kept her waiting—stewing—in his outer office for nearly an hour. She'd turned down three offers of coffee from his efficient, bookish secretary, avoiding eye contact with a vengeance.

She'd decided it would be cowardly to call and cancel her appointment, for if there was one thing a Meadows was not, it was cowardly. She didn't like to think what people called *some* of the Meadowses, although nuts came to mind. Of course, Minny was completely good-hearted, and like it or not, her dream readings, as she called them— predicting futures, loves and financial well-being for her handful of loyal clients—had helped out with Angela's college tuition. For this, Angela was grateful and ferociously protective.

There had been those who'd called her father lazy and good-for-nothing. However, Angela preferred to remember him as a warm generous romantic who'd loved his wife and daughter, but perhaps wasn't the greatest farmer in the world. Dan Meadows had died young and poor, and Angela and Minny still mourned his passing.

That had been when Angela was eighteen. Now, after six years of part-time jobs and college classes, Angela had her degree, and by heaven, she planned to succeed at the business she'd started! She'd won the Wichita State University's Young Entrepreneur award for her idea of a store consisting exclusively of sturdy, colorful, space-saving and space-expanding containers. Inner Space, as she'd dubbed it, had been judged the "best plan for a new company."

She'd been in her shop for six months. It had taken all their money and all Angela's time. For what seemed like years, she'd had no social life, no clothes, not even much sleep. And now, she was about to be lambasted by a snobbish, wealthy playboy whose brains—if the tabloids were to be believed—resided primarily in his trousers. Life, to use a cliché, wasn't fair!

Angela recrossed her legs again and nervously fiddled with the lapel of her blue jacket. She had a horrible urge to run to the ladies' room to reassure herself that she hadn't chewed off all her lipstick, but she couldn't risk being gone when Mr. Heaven's Gift to Chocolate Eaters freed up some time to rake her over the coals. Why she even cared if she had lipstick on was beyond her. No doubt it was her fierce pride, the same pride that insisted she come here to be personally fired rather than quietly slink away into the night, forever remembered by Tarrant Seaton as "one of those two weirdos in The Plethora."

"Miss Meadows?"

Angela's gaze flew to the woman behind the wide oak desk, a desk suspiciously clear of work. Angela had to wonder if Tarrant was really anything but a carousing figurehead for Delila's Delights. "Yes?" she said at last, her voice a little tight.

"Mr. Seaton will see you now."

Angela was puzzled. She'd heard no intercom buzz the message. Getting to her feet and retrieving her briefcase, she headed across the tawny carpeting toward the double mahogany doors. She couldn't help but think that this waiting game had been planned. Her nagging distrust didn't make her feel any kindlier toward the man on the other side of those intimidating doors.

For such big heavy doors, they opened with ease as her hands barely grazed the brass knobs. When they'd swung wide, she found herself standing in the entrance of a very masculine inner sanctum that oozed wealth. The floor was inlaid wood, reflecting the sunshine streaming through a bank of high arched windows a good forty feet away. An antique Sarouk rug of maroon, cobalt blue and wine swathed the center of the room. The marble fireplace to her left was large enough to stand in. Above it hung a striking collection of Western American watercolors. On her right, the wood-paneled wall was filled with glass-fronted bookshelves, overflowing with books. This surprised Angela; she never thought of the Prince of Delights as a man with a contemplative, literary side. Probably just his decorator's idea for detailing the room, she decided.

Tarrant Seaton, her immediate problem, was sitting behind a huge carved cherry desk. He'd removed his coat and loosened his tie. He was on the phone, his wide brow beetled in either thought or exasperation. As she closed the door, he glanced up, his shadowed eyes stabbing her for one annoyed second before he looked back down at the file folder lying open on his desk. "Harry, I realize that the mistake wasn't all your fault, but your Detroit operation has to start meeting deadlines. Don't apologize—just do it. And I need those latest cost figures—" he gave his wrist an irritated jerk so that he could see his watch, which Angela guessed was solid gold "—by eleven. All right, talk to you later."

He settled the receiver in its cradle with less rancor than she would have expected, considering his tone, then sat back and closed his eyes. He exhaled slowly, as though regaining his calm, before directing his attention to Angela. When he did, his expression darkened even further.

"Miss Meadows." It wasn't a question.

She drew back her shoulders in subconscious rebellion. The unruly urge to ask for a blindfold and a cigarette sped through her mind, and she was hard put not to voice it. No, an attempt to lighten the situation wouldn't do. He didn't appear to be a man of much humor—unless he was laughing *at* someone. She managed to clear her throat of the lump that had formed there. "Mr. Seaton," she returned as coolly as she could manage. It was not a question, either.

He inclined his handsome head toward one of two rosewood armchairs on her side of the desk. "Have a seat, Miss Meadows."

She was taken aback. She'd figured he'd toss her out on her ear before she could get that far into the room. Hiding her trepidation, as well as her surprise, she crossed the glistening wood, her heels marking her passing with a rapid tap-tap-tap. When she reached the rug, the room fell into a palpable silence. Seating herself, she placed the brief-case on the floor, then folded her hands in her lap, resisting the desire to clench her fingers together to keep them from shaking.

He'd scowled at her every step of the way. Now he stood up and retrieved his tan suitcoat—hand-stitched, Angela noticed, calculating that it had probably cost him more than her whole wardrobe. Maybe even more than her car.

After he'd slipped it on, he ambled around his desk, no small feat in itself, and then, to her surprise, propped a lean hip on its edge. Slipping his hands into the pockets of his slacks, he looked down at her. She had to admit he dressed with impressive taste, from his silk tie to his precisely polished wing tips. She was terribly outclassed as far as money was concerned, but Angela refused to be intimidated by either his good looks or the costly surroundings, although she was sure the great Tarrant Seaton was banking on that.

She met his challenge—narrowed gaze for narrowed gaze, dry smile for dry smile. Inwardly Angela cringed, recalling yesterday's fiasco. But when he hadn't said anything after a full minute, she finally decided she'd had enough of his silent browbeating. Stiff-lipped, she informed him, "I have a shop to run, Mr. Seaton. Our appointment was for an hour ago. Rather than walk out on you, as I could have, I waited. It's your affair if you've chosen not to hire me, but I don't have time to play juvenile games. Either fire me or let's get on with business."

His dark eyes roamed over her for an instant more, his level gaze revealing nothing of what was going on in his mind. Then, with a ridiculing twist of his lip, he inquired, "*My* juvenile games, Miss Meadows?"

Angela swallowed. His question dripped with sarcasm. But she forced herself to meet his stare as her pride butted up against her good sense. She'd planned to apologize for the incident at the restaurant, to tell him that most of the time Minny's predictions had merely been a matter of misinterpreting her muddled dreams, coming to nothing. But his superior attitude and grating sarcasm had made that impossible. The last thing in the world she planned to do now was make excuses for her mother's behavior to this . . . this insolent bully.

"Then I'm fired?" she asked, careful not to let any of her feelings show.

He gave her another long, contemptuous look, which she refused to squirm beneath. "Nothing would please me more, Miss Meadows," he finally admitted, his face drawn in uncompromising lines.

Why did she feel a "but" coming? She held her breath.

"But," he continued, "it was my mother's decision to hire you, and I don't intend to go against her wishes. She ran this company for over twenty years without my help, and I won't insult her business acumen by countermanding her orders. Though," he added with obvious acrimony, "I believe, in this case, she was wrong."

"You have a right to your opinion," Angela replied, her tone as chilly as his, though if the truth be known, she was dumbfounded. He wasn't firing her!

"Just so we understand each other."

"We do," she assured him, maintaining her outward calm. "So with that settled, perhaps you should have someone show me the plant."

He nodded curtly, and his face betrayed little emotion. He was clearly unhappy about being stuck with her, and this revelation suddenly made Angela feel good, victorious even. Her expression grew dangerously close to smug.

"It's been...nice meeting you, Mr. Seaton," she lied. "I'll try not to disturb you any more than necessary."

He smiled, too. But his was the same scornful smile he'd directed at her in the restaurant, not a reassuring look to say the least. "Miss Meadows, let's be clear on one thing." He stood, towering over her. "You won't disturb me, no matter how hard you try. I find your stratagem of using your mother to 'predict' a marriage between ourselves to be unique, but far from disturbing. I'm no babe in the woods, Miss Meadows. Women more worldly than you have tried tricking me into matrimony. None have succeeded."

Angela knew about his reputation with women. His picture was regularly emblazoned across the front pages of the tabloids. Not that she actually read the stories, just absently scanned them in grocery stores. The most recent photo display had shown him escorting one glamorous starlet after another during his recent California visit. And here he stood, blatantly implying that these women had made passes at *him* rather than the other way around!

Angela bristled. What an overbearing, conceited oaf! Pushing up from a chair that had been every bit as cold and inhospitable as the man before her, she retorted, "I can only hope all those women who supposedly want to marry you realize their good fortune in not succeeding!" Bending to retrieve her briefcase, she added hotly, "And just for the record, I would never stoop so low to catch a man—especially one as arrogant and self-centered as you are, Mr. Seaton!"

Turning abruptly, she'd planned to stride haughtily away from him, but as fate would have it, she caught her heel in the carpet and tumbled across the arm of the chair, upending herself. One hand slammed the floor; the other landed on her toppled briefcase.

"Oh, jeez!" she cried, the blood rushing to her head. This was not the disdainful exit she'd envisioned. She heard Tarrant Seaton clear his throat, and she would have bet big money that the insufferable lout was smothering a laugh!

"Miss Meadows," he asked from behind her. "Do you need any help?"

"No!" She pushed herself backward until her feet were on the floor. "No, don't bother," she wheezed. "I'm ... fine."

Even with her breathless protest, she felt his hand encircle her elbow, helping her balance until she was once again standing on her own. Their eyes met for the briefest, most appalling second, and she murmured, "I'll just be going now."

Out of the corner of her eye, she could see him pick up her briefcase. "Here," he said, extending it toward her.

She grabbed it and mumbled something. He would probably assume she was thanking him, but did it really matter what she said at this point? As she made a beeline for the exit, she was distressed to hear him call her name. She pretended not to hear, but when he repeated it for the third time, he also took hold of her arm. She really had no choice but to acknowledge his presence.

"What is it?" she snapped, reluctantly facing him. Her cheeks were hot, and she was sure that not only was she a fiery red, but her hair had all the well-groomed allure of someone who'd wandered into a wind tunnel. "Really, Mr. Seaton, I'm in quite a hurry."

"Haven't you forgotten something, Miss Meadows?" he asked coolly, his eyes betraying amusement at her expense.

"No. I think I've fallen over just about everything I care to."

He seemed to struggle with a grin. "That's heartening news. I mean, don't you want to tour the plant?"

She grimaced. She'd totally lost her wits, it appeared. Pushing back a shock of curls that rested across her nose, she nodded. "Of course. I—I was just about to remind you."

"Oh? Forgive me for blundering in. I'll have my plant manager, Marge Collins, meet you in the employees' lounge." He'd begun to guide her toward the door when he added, "By the way, Miss Meadows..."

When they'd reached the exit and he had said no more, she cautiously faced him again. Exasperated, she asked, "By the way *what*, Mr. Seaton?"

"It's Tuesday, Miss Meadows, and your panties read Wednesday. If you're going to work for me, you'll need to show more attention to detail."

She gaped at him, mortified. It would have been kinder if he'd just shot her! Trembling with rage, she gathered a measure of her poise and pinned him with a disgusted stare. "I would rather be a day ahead, Mr. Seaton, than...than a horse's behind!"

The slamming of his elegant doors echoed, a testament to her burning indignation. As she fled, Angela couldn't help but recall him as he'd looked when she uttered her last words—very tall, very polished and very grim.

CHAPTER TWO

TARRANT RAN INTO Marge Collins on his way into the employee cafeteria and stopped to talk to her. "Marge. How did it go with that Meadows person this morning?"

Marge, a woman in her mid-fifties, wearing her platinum hair pulled severely back and a gray suit that was equally severe, smiled, belying her tough facade. "That little thing?" she inquired huskily. "Why, when I saw her I couldn't believe she was old enough to have any ideas about how to dress herself, let alone organize this old barn." She shrugged. "No offense, Tarrant, but this factory is a big, waste-making—"

Tarrant waved off her apology, grinning. "I know all about the place, Marge. That's why Mother wants the storage space updated. So, what do you think of Miss Meadows?"

Marge removed her silver-framed glasses and whipped a lacy handkerchief out of her sleeve to polish them. "She was quiet. Took lots of notes. Said she'd have some recommendations by Monday. Asked good questions."

"What's your gut feeling?"

Marge replaced her glasses. "Like her." She nodded curtly. "I do, Tarrant. I think she's got what it takes."

A reflective frown marred his clean-cut features.

"Why? Don't you?"

One well-defined brow lifted speculatively, but other than that Tarrant's expression gave away none of his thoughts. "If Mother wants to give her a chance, I won't interfere."

Marge patted his arm. "Well, when you took over as marketing director for Delila's Delights nine years ago, I wasn't too sure about you, either. You were a brash young pup of twenty-three with nothing going for you but a shiny new MBA...."

"And a mother who owned the company," he added with a grin.

Marge cocked her head and eyed him critically. "I hope you're not still worried that people think you can't handle the job, that you just got it because you're Delila's only son. That silly notion has been proven wrong time and time again."

He wagged a finger at her. "Still the mother hen, Marge?" The lazy nonchalance in his voice served to relax the woman's features.

"Well, I think all our stockholders would have to admit that your mother was a smart cookie to hire you. Even so, when she gave you the presidency two years later, I thought Delila had gone mad, handing you a million-dollar business." She grinned up at him, her expression close to maternal. "But look at you, Tarrant. Chief executive of what's now the second-largest gourmet-chocolate company in the country, and it's still growing." She laughed wryly. "So, as far as Miss Meadows's abilities go, I'll say the same thing Delila said about you, 'Let's give the kid a shot.'"

A scowl touched his brows and he sighed. "I suppose having Miss Meadows draw up a few ideas can't bankrupt us."

Marge smiled approvingly. "There's a good boy."

"Marge," Tarrant warned, his expression softening. "Don't let the troops hear you call me that. They'll think I'm not the ogre I've built myself up to be."

She looked around, then confided, "Yeah? Well, I hate to tell you, Tarrant, but if you want a reputation as an ogre, you'll have to quit eating lunch with the employees. It tends to raise morale, not strike terror in their hearts."

He put an arm about her shoulders. "Speaking of lunch, have you eaten?"

She shook her head. "I've got a date with a handsome Wichita lawyer."

"Husbands. They steal all my fun."

She laughed. "That's not what I've heard."

Casting her a dubious look, he moved toward the lunchroom. "Don't believe everything you hear."

Her laughter chased him into the cafeteria, where the din of clattering plates and people enjoying their lunch break surrounded him. As he started across the room, there was a tug on his sleeve. Turning, he saw the peculiar woman from The Plethora, the older one. She was dressed in a green-and-white caftan, and her black hair, streaked with gray, was piled on top of her head in a fanciful sculpture reminiscent of a swirled mound of ice cream.

"Hello there, son." She smiled sweetly. "I hope you don't mind my calling you son. After all, it's only a matter of time before you will be—my son, that is."

"What are you doing here, Mrs. Meadows?" he asked curtly.

Her fingers fluttered momentarily before they seemed to find their purpose. With one hand lifted high, she pointed. "I brought Angela her lunch. Her usual—Twinkies, crunchy peanut butter sandwich, herbal tea. See? She's right over there. Third table down, with those girls in white smocks." Taking one of his large hands into hers, she urged, "Why don't you go over and sit with her? She seemed a little down. I know seeing you would perk her right up."

"You think so?" he asked, sarcasm staining his voice.

She seemed incredulous. "Why, of course. Any bride would be delighted to see her groom." She smiled again, her eyes shining. "When I had my dream, I had no idea you'd be so handsome, son."

"You're too kind, Mrs. Meadows." Withdrawing his hand from hers, he added dryly, "It would be my pleasure to join your daughter for lunch. I believe we do have...more to discuss." His polite smile had gone hard. "If you'll excuse me, Mrs. Meadows?"

"Oh," she said with a giggle, "call me Minny. I mean, after all—"

"How generous of you, Minny," he interrupted, effectively cutting her off.

As he began to move away, Minny grabbed his sleeve again. "Son," she said, her features growing sober, "did you know you have a muscle jumping in your jaw? Is everything all right? You seem a little tense." She reached up to indicate the jerking muscle, but he stepped aside, avoiding her touch.

"I can't imagine why I'd be tense, Mrs. Meadows. Happily engaged as I am."

Her smile returned, but she made a tsking sound at him. "Minny, remember? Call me Minny, son. And you might want to invest in a good memory class. You're a tiny bit forgetful."

"I'll keep it in mind." With a curt nod toward the small woman who resembled a mutant butterfly, he stalked over toward the lunch line.

"Oh, look who's coming," a pretty redhead whispered loudly to her companion, pulling off her hair net and stuffing it into her smock pocket. Angela glanced up from her sandwich and caught the redhead gesturing toward someone behind Angela's back. "Mr. Seaton!"

The other woman, plump and freckle-faced, looked up, squeaking, "Oh, gracious! He's coming right here!" She'd already removed her hair net, and was attempting to tame her flyaway blond hair.

Angela felt the peanut butter become a barricade in her throat. She tried to swallow, but it refused to budge. *Here? Lord help her! Please! Not so soon after the "horse's behind" remark.* What could possibly have possessed her to blurt out something that rude? And to the company's president, yet! Rarely did she completely lose her temper, but there was just something about Tarrant Seaton that brought out her stubborn hotheaded side. She regretted her unflattering retort, but there was little she could do about it now—except stay out of his way.

She took a swig of her tea, now tepid, forcing the peanut butter down.

"Hello, ladies."

She heard the smooth deep voice she recognized as Tarrant's, and hunched low in her seat, taking an undue interest in how Twinkies were sealed into their packages. She carefully scrutinized every crease and fold, praying fervently that he would pass her table by.

"May I join you?" he queried pleasantly, dashing Angela's hopes.

Giggles met his request. "Sure, Tarr—er, Mr. Seaton," the freckle-faced woman replied.

Unfortunately, he took the empty seat beside Angela, and even more unfortunately, he noticed her. "Well, hello there, Miss Meadows. This is a coincidence."

She pressed her lips together and tore into her Twinkies.

"What?" he asked as he settled into his chair, his closeness irksome, his cologne hypnotic. "I didn't quite catch that."

She gave up. Apparently he was going to insist that she acknowledge him, so she darted a sidelong look in the vicinity of his square-cut chin, with its much photographed cleft. It surprised her that she recalled that chin so vividly from scratchy newspaper photos, and she berated herself for cluttering her mind with such frivolous trivia. Averting her gaze, she mumbled, "Hello—"

The redhead broke in. "Mr. Seaton, I love the new Honey Bundles. They're *awesome.*"

Tarrant graced her with a rakish flash of teeth that made her blush. "Thank you... Marty, is it?"

Marty fairly glowed with delight. "Yes, sir. Marty Rainwater. Caramel-nut section."

"Well, thank you, Marty. The Honey Bundles are the result of our employee idea program. Karen Mergunson got a five-hundred-dollar bonus for making the suggestion that led to their development."

"Wow! Karen's lucky," Marty exclaimed with melodramatic relish, clasping her hands to her ample bosom.

Tarrant's deep chuckle irritated Angela. "You could win, too, Marty," he went on. "It just takes a good idea."

"Oh, I've got *lots* of awesome ideas... sir."

Angela glanced at the redhead, getting the distinct feeling that her remark had not been referring to the subject of candy. While Marty preened before Tarrant, Angela closed her eyes, flinching at having to witness such a blatant come-on. Maybe it was true. Maybe Tarrant Seaton did get propositions like this from women all the time. If so, no wonder he had an ego the size of a barn!

Angela heard Tarrant shift in his seat. She felt a shiver rise from the base of her spine and knew he was looking at her. "What do you think of our new Honey Bundles, *darling?*"

The last word had been uttered in a sexy drawl. Angela's eyes flew open with shock, and the Twinkie she'd been about to bite into fell to her lunch tray.

Tarrant chuckled devilishly, turning to face the other young women, who had grown still—as had another cluster of female employees farther down the table, hanging on their employer's every word. "Oh, didn't Angela tell you?" Tarrant asked by way of explanation. "Angela and I are to be married. I understand her mother dreamed it."

Angela knew she must be imagining it, but all two-hundred-odd sets of eyes in the cafeteria seemed to be glued on her at this moment.

Unrelenting, Tarrant want on, "I was surprised when I first heard. But now that I think about it, I'm flattered." Deliberately he lifted his coffee to his lips, allowing the uncomfortable pause to grow burdensome. The room fell deadly silent when he finally spoke again. "Wouldn't you be flattered, Marty, if some stranger came up and told you that you were going to marry her son?"

It took the startled redhead a minute to find her voice. Then she blurted, "I—I don't think so. I think I'd be mad, Mr. Seaton." She glared at Angela. "I'd feel tricked and trapped is what I think."

"Oh? Well, that's a thought." Tarrant sounded genuinely surprised, managing to mask the churlishness Angela was certain had prompted this whole conversation.

Since Angela was well aware that his apparent approval of the idea of marrying her was an act, she had a rebellious urge to dump her tea in his lap. This was the vilest revenge he could have gotten on her. She had to work among these people for weeks! Now everyone would know about her mother's prediction. They'd poke fun at Angela. Even if some of them meant only good-natured ribbing, it would still hurt. She'd never hear the end of it, not at the factory, or even in Seatonville. Known as a bedroom community just north of Wichita, Seatonville wasn't that big a town. Angela was so humiliated she wanted to scream—and then just evaporate.

"What do you think, Angela? Should I be flattered? Or angry?" His question held a barely detectable edge that made her wince.

There was little to do but respond. Everybody within prodding distance was now all ears. She took a deep breath before turning to confront him. He eyed her steadily, the dark brilliance of his gaze throwing off challenging sparks that almost seared her flesh. But his thick black lashes shielded that inimical look from the others. He appeared the callow innocent here, and she, the big bad wolf! Her cheeks began to blaze, and it took a great deal of restraint to keep from slapping the manipulative, self-serving brute across his handsome face.

He was being vastly unfair. Yet ironically, the unjustness of the situation became a sort of catalyst, bolstering her courage. She vowed silently that Tarrant Seaton would learn Angela Meadows was not one to take such tyrannical treatment lying down. Keeping her voice steady, she said, "You're quite the humorous maggot, aren't you?"

"You mean 'magnate,'" he corrected with a sly crook of his lips.

Lifting her tray, she rose and turned away, assuring him over her shoulder, "No, *darling*, I don't." It gave her some satisfaction to notice his smile waver.

"So, you're gonna marry Mr. Seaton?" Marty chided maliciously when she ran into Angela in the ladies' room just outside the lunchroom.

Angela went on washing her hands as Marty stuffed her red curls back under her hair net. "Didn't you hear me?" she persisted, turning to block Angela's path.

Angela gave her a level look and held up her wet hands. "Do you mind? I need a towel."

The redhead frowned, reluctantly moving aside, but she didn't let it go. "You know, honey, Mr. Seaton's pretty sharp. He'd never fall for a stupid trick like that.... Dreams yet!" she chortled, shaking her head. "Some women amaze me. What gall!"

Angela dropped her paper towel into the waste receptacle before responding to the woman's unkind remarks. With a carefully closed expression, Angela suggested, "Don't you mean *awesome* gall?"

As the redhead stared daggers at her, Angela forced herself to walk casually out of the room, positive the harassing had only begun—thanks to one Pulitzer Prize-winning jerk!

ANGELA WAS BEAT. She just wanted to crawl into a hot tub and soak for the rest of her natural life. But she had one more thing to do before she could divest herself of both the day's clothes and cares, though she doubted she'd be able to rid herself completely of the latter. She'd endured ribbing all afternoon. Even the austere Mrs. Collins had eyed her strangely when they'd resumed their tour of the factory.

Angela sighed and turned her decrepit old clunker away from Seatonville. She'd promised to meet with Delila Seaton at five o'clock to have a look around the mansion. She'd been so excited about getting the job, she hadn't stopped to consider how much time checking the factory would take, let alone the mansion. She hoped she'd be able to get by with merely a discussion of Mrs. Seaton's remodeling needs, and that she'd be allowed to put off the actual inspection of the sixty-four room residence until tomorrow.

At the gate, the security guard waved her through, since she had an appointment. In her rearview mirror she watched as the twelve-foot-high iron portals swung shut. She switched her gaze ahead along the ribbon of pavement that wended its way among towering conifers—firs, pines and other rarer trees. It seemed as though the entire road was edged with flower beds and shrubs, dynamic in their arrangement. The delicate colors of the meandering beds were sharpened and artfully defined by the darker arboreal background. One hundred years ago, the place had been little more than flat dusty prairie, and Angela had to marvel at the primeval lushness of the Seaton family home, known as Havenhearth.

She couldn't see the mansion yet, but she'd seen photographs of it. The neo-Georgian-columned facade had been described in *Architectural Digest* as "the most legendary home in the Midwest."

Angela might have been hired just to redesign storage space; still, it was a plum assignment and she knew it. As the story went, Noah Seaton, who had a penchant for assisting struggling new businesses, became enamored of the lovely young Delila Holmes and had given her a loan to begin her chocolate business. He had won her heart several years later.

Delila Seaton carried on her husband's philanthropic inclinations. Though Noah had died ten years ago, Angela passed him a silent thank-you. She didn't want to feel unkindly toward such a wonderful man's son, or such a wonderful woman's son, for that matter. But right now, *unkind* thoughts were the only sort she could conjure up for Tarrant Seaton. She desperately hoped she wouldn't run into him while she was here. She reassured herself that he'd probably remain at the office until at least six o'clock, so she'd try to be good and gone by then.

Rounding a stand of bald cypress, she saw the great house, its whiteness glowing pearlescent in the late-afternoon sun. Stories about the lush landscaping had reached mythical proportions, but had been far from overstated. Hundreds of varieties of flowers and blossoming shrubs, a month away from full radiant bloom, embraced the house and the terrace that led down to a small lake fronting the mansion. The calm water reflected the noble lines and elegant proportions of Havenhearth.

Seven exquisite swans floated over the blue-green surface, lending a fantastical quality to the scene. Angela held her breath at the sedate charm of the place, once again realizing the magnitude of her good fortune in being selected to modernize the storage space here. She'd probably never even see Delila; instead, she'd be relegated to basements, attics and pantries. But then, she'd also be a comfortable distance from the arrogant master of the mansion. As she maneuvered her old car into the circular driveway and pulled to a stop, she decided that not having to set eyes on Tarrant Seaton was, in itself, all the bonus she could hope for.

Just as she stepped onto the pavement, the roar of a powerful engine caught her attention, and she almost gave way to a self-protective impulse to leap back into her car when a silver Lamborghini roared to a halt inches from her rear bumper. She clamped her jaws together tightly, hating her bad timing. Everyone in Seatonville recognized that luxury sports car as belonging to the great and powerful Wizard of Oohs and Ahs, the so-called Prince of Delights.

She steeled herself for trouble as Tarrant climbed out of the car, looking much too fresh for five in the afternoon. He gave her a quick, rankling once-over, then settled his gaze on her car, a mechanical refugee from a junkyard. She eyed him narrowly, daring him to make a derisive remark. Irked by his silence, she accused, "You nearly hit me, you know."

His glance flicked to her with a mixture of amusement and surprise. "I don't think so."

"Well, I do," she protested, annoyed that he was laughing at her again.

His lips twisted in a grin. "This won't be the first time we've disagreed." He shut the door of his car, and Angela noticed it took practically no effort to do so—not like her car door, which needed a mighty shove accompanied by a very unladylike grunt. With vexation pumping adrenaline through her, she decided she could lift an elephant if she had to and gave her door a vigorous push. Still, without the usual grunt, she didn't quite accomplish her objective. "Rats," she muttered between tight lips.

Shaking his head at her ineptness, he ambled over, opened the door, then reclosed it securely. In the process, one of her retreads went flat.

"Oh, that's just fine," she moaned.

"Nice car," he remarked dryly. "That tire-flattening option is a feature I hadn't heard of."

"You're horribly funny."

"I know. You've told me that before," he reminded her. "Remember me? The humorous maggot?"

She ignored the remark, mumbling to herself, "What am I going to do?"

"Junk it."

She lifted her gaze from her deflated tire and exhaled tiredly. "We don't all have the resources to throw away something just because it isn't perfect anymore."

His chuckle was sardonic. "That car might have been perfect once, but it was before you were born." He stooped to examine the tire. "I'll have this repaired for you before you leave."

She frowned, not sure she wanted his charity. "I couldn't let you do that."

He looked up at her, his expression set. "I closed the blasted door. I'll fix the blasted tire. Now, what are you doing here? And don't tell me it's to discuss the guest list for the wedding. I'm not in the mood for games."

When he'd unfolded himself to his full menacing height, Angela squared her shoulders defensively. "Don't be insulting. I have an appointment with Mrs. Seaton—about reorganizing storage space in the mansion."

He eyed her with misgiving, but didn't question her further. Nodding at the double entry, he said, "I'll show you where to find her."

"Don't bother." Angela sped around the front of her disabled vehicle. "Don't you have to park your car in a garage or a vault or someplace?"

"Chauncey will do it."

She stopped and turned back. "Why? Is your aim so bad you can't get it in?"

His lips twitched with wicked humor, and she knew why. Her innocent remark had come out sounding decidedly off-color.

"Would you care to try that again?" he asked.

She swallowed hard and spun on her heel, heading away from him. To her distress, he followed. At the door, she searched in vain for either a knocker or a doorbell. Feeling stupid, she knocked. Her efforts were laughably ineffectual, her bare hand making hardly a sound on the thick solid wood door. There was little hope that anybody inside had heard it.

After an agonizing few moments, while Tarrant stood right behind her, she finally had to give up. With grave reluctance she faced him. "All right," she sighed, "how do I let someone know I'm here?"

Tarrant stepped up and threw a switch cleverly disguised in the woodwork. "Alexander? I have a guest at the door."

"Yes, sir," came the immediate reply.

"It'll only be a minute," Tarrant explained, lounging against the wall looking as self-assured and handsome as ever. It galled her to realize he was enjoying himself immensely. "How was I supposed to know that was there?" she asked, indignant.

He indicated a hidden camera up near the roof to their left. "Someone would have inquired, had I not been with you. Since I was here, Alexander knew I had matters in hand."

"Oh, Alexander knew that, did he?" She fixed him with the glower usually reserved for stubborn shower-curtain mildew. "Then I have both you and Alexander to thank for my being late to see your mother."

A moment later, the door opened, and a tall man dressed impeccably in black ushered them in.

The foyer was at least twenty-five feet square, with a curving staircase, oak paneling and marble floors setting such a dramatic tone that the sight took Angela's breath away. A crystal chandelier hung low, accentuating the artistic curve of the staircase. Within that curve, directly below the chandelier, sat an oaken drum table. It held a lavish arrangement of silk flowers and greenery, which emphasized the room's color scheme—the rich glowing wood, the warm ruby carpeting and the antique white of the floor and high-beamed ceiling.

"Alexander, Miss Meadows says she had an appointment with Mrs. Seaton. Pat her down for weapons and show her to the library."

"Yes, sir." With a gloved hand Alexander indicated the way. "If you'll follow me, miss?"

Though Alexander's expression remained serious, Angela could tell by the tone of Tarrant's voice that the "pat her down" remark had been a joke, however impudent. Her host was goading her. Again, to show her appreciation for his caustic sense of humor, she tossed him one last scornful glare.

Tarrant merely inclined his head in a mocking gesture of farewell and strolled away.

CHAPTER THREE

As DELILA SEATON conversed quietly with Alexander, Angela took a moment to survey both her hostess and the imposing room in which she sat. Delila, delicately beautiful at fifty-five, wore a floor-length dress made of fine linen batiste, its cuffs, collar and hem trimmed with lace. Her hair was the color of champagne, and she wore it bobbed in a close-fitting cap. She wore no jewelry, except a simple gold ring on her left hand. As she spoke to Alexander, Angela could hear the huskiness of her voice, pleasant yet authoritative. She found herself drawn to the woman, even if Delila did resemble her son a bit too much around the mouth.

Allowing her gaze to wander about the room, she was again struck by the grandeur of the place. Though the library was a large room, it exuded an intimate warmth, from the well-stocked bookshelves to the dusty rose of the walls and draperies. The wood trim was painted a soft flax color, and the chandelier was of gleaming polished brass. A breakfront stood against the wall opposite the bookshelves. It contained an intriguing variety of antiques: a mother-of-pearl stallion, a jade leopard and myriad brass maritime devices.

A rose, moss and gold Sultanabad rug hugged the wood floor and served to accentuate the gray-green damask of the contemporary sofa and armchairs. The end tables were of satinwood, as was the Baker tray table, on which the silver tea service sat.

The picture window at the back of the room overlooked a stone patio with a three-tiered fountain as its centerpiece. Beyond the patio glimmered the pristine water of a swimming pool that had been landscaped to look like a natural pond. Atop a diving board stood Tarrant Seaton, preparing to dive. Thighs bunched and calf muscles bulged as he tensed with the effort of his upward launch and executed a flawless back flip that made Angela gasp.

Both Delila and Alexander looked her way. "Is everything all right, my dear?" Delila asked softly.

Angela blanched. "I..." She nodded. "Your son nearly hit his head on the diving board." She bit her lip, hoping Delila didn't think she'd been ogling.

The older woman glanced out the window. "Oh? Don't fret about Tarrant, my dear. He's quite a good diver. But I know what you mean. I used to get terribly upset watching him." Turning back to Angela, she shrugged elegantly. "I simply don't watch anymore."

Angela's smile was weak. *Easier said than done,* she mused silently, but she merely said, "I'm sorry for disturbing you."

"Oh, you didn't disturb us at all," Delila assured her, dismissing Alexander with a nod. "As a matter of fact, I was about to suggest that you join Tarrant and me for dinner. Though I have to go out later this evening, I can trust him to show you the storage areas that are in need of remodeling. I have a great number of projects on hold, and I need that work done as quickly as possible." She smiled benignly. "What do you say?"

Angela had never been so smoothly coerced in her life. Delila's invitation had been nothing short of a direct order, but she'd done it with such finesse that Angela couldn't say no—even though it meant another run-in with Tarrant Seaton.

Just then, the man darkening her thoughts completed a perfect double flip. Unaccountably Angela's heart did, too. She had to admit that he really was wonderful to look at. To avoid any further view of him, she lowered her gaze to her clenched fists. She didn't even like the man, for heaven's sake!

"Well, my dear," Delila prodded. "What do you think of my plan—dinner and a tour of the house?"

Angela composed her expression and smiled, though she had no love for the idea. She was worn out, and the prospect of spending one more instant with Delila's son was unwelcome. "Why, it sounds lovely, Mrs. Seaton," she heard herself lie.

THE APRIL DAY was unusually warm and a welcome change. With the temperature hovering around eighty, even at half-past five, Angela was delighted to discover they were going to eat on the mansion's sunny patio. Then she realized that Tarrant would be joining them—in his bathing gear.

The dinner progressed well. Angela found herself laughing at Tarrant's wry wit, and she was amazed at herself. He exuded an easy charm, flashed a quick smile and lulled one into a cozy camaraderie with his deep pleasing voice. Angela, of course, had built up an impervious resistance to him since that day in the restaurant when he'd been so unforgivably disdainful. But she could see how other, more susceptible women might succumb to him. Unfortunately, every time he said something that struck her as clever and she chanced to smile his way, she was confronted by his attire—or lack of it—and blushed furiously.

From the amusement twinkling in Tarrant's eyes, she could tell he was enjoying her discomfort. No doubt he was paying her back for what he thought she'd engineered in the restaurant.

"My dear," Delila finally noted, "you must be quite sensitive to the sun. You're getting a little pink."

Stalling, Angela pretended to sip some water and tried to decide how to explain her flushed face.

"Well, in deference to your delicate skin," Delila went on, replacing her teacup in its saucer, "I think it's time we went inside. And Tarrant, dear, put on some clothes. We don't want our guest to think we're barbarians, do we?"

He grinned at his mother, and Angela's gaze was drawn, yet again, to the single, slashing dimple that indented his left cheek. She turned away from it, though its impact continued to adversely affect the pit of her stomach.

"I don't think anything I wear could sway Miss Meadows's opinion of me," Tarrant remarked, shooting a glance toward Angela. "Would it, Miss Meadows?"

In the depths of his eyes she saw the cynicism she was growing accustomed to. His look told her that he believed her to be a scheming, money-hungry opportunist, and that his mode of attire would have no effect on her blackhearted motives.

Angela returned his falsely pleasant expression with one of her own. "You're absolutely right, Mr. Seaton."

The smile that crooked his lips was sardonic, affording her another glimpse of his bothersome dimple. "There, you see, Mother," he said, pushing himself up from the table. "All your worry for nothing." Rounding the table, he kissed Delila on the cheek. With his hands on her shoulders, he looked across the table at Angela. "I'll slip into something less barbaric and meet you in the kitchen in fifteen minutes.''

Delila laughed and patted her son's hand. "You're such a fool, dear.''

You're such a conniving pain! Angela thought darkly.

As Tarrant chuckled for his mother's benefit, he caught Angela's gaze in the vise of his own. "I shall always be a fool for you, Mother,'' he murmured. Then he straightened and strolled away, but not before Angela received his telegraphed message. Tarrant Holmes Seaton, Prince of Delights and hotshot tycoon, would *never* be a fool for a devious little mantrap like Angela Meadows.

Fifteen minutes later, as he'd promised, Tarrant appeared in the kitchen doorway, freshly showered and clad in linen slacks and a cotton-knit sweater. So correctly careless was he in his calfskin loafers and no socks, that Angela couldn't help but eye him with some hostility. Why did he have to look this attractive when she felt as though she'd been dragged around a dusty floor on the end of a mop handle? It had been a long day for her, and it was far from over. She had a nagging feeling that the worst was yet to come.

Grabbing up her notebook, she fairly groaned, "I'm very tired, Mr. Seaton. Could we make this quick?''

"Have a hard day at the office?'' His voice was taunting, though his handsome face was the picture of concern.

She stiffened with indignation. Her "hard day at the office'' had been entirely his fault, and he knew it! "Why don't you become a stand-up comic?'' she snapped. "That way you could annoy hundreds of people at a time.''

His lips twitched. She couldn't tell if he was laughing at her or if he was amused because he found her comeback clever. "I see we get cranky when we're not getting our way," he observed. "Not a very professional attitude, Miss Meadows."

She almost choked. How dared he treat her with such shabby condescension? Well, if he expected the satisfaction of bullying her into quitting, then he had vastly underestimated her! She needed this job, and she was sticking it out, come hell—in the insufferable incarnation of Tarrant Seaton—or high water! Counting silently to ten, she managed to compose her voice. "If you'd rather, you can send Alexander with me. As a matter of fact, I'd prefer Alexander."

"After six on Tuesdays, Alexander has the evenings off."

He moved up beside her, and she could detect the subtle tang of his cologne. Trying to ignore the captivating scent, she muttered, "Lucky Alexander."

Passing her a reserved half smile that told her he'd heard her remark, he said, "Since we seem to be stuck with each other, Miss Meadows, where would you like to start?"

She avoided looking at him. "The basement?"

He indicated a door. "After you."

A bank of lights went on as she descended the staircase into a morass of hallways and darkened rooms, some filled with boxes and crates, some dank and barren. Neither Tarrant nor Angela spoke as she strolled slowly around, taking notes and making quick sketches. From the things Mrs. Seaton had told her, she had some idea of the work required, but now, seeing the size and condition of these rooms, Angela's mind whirled with all that needed to be done.

Tarrant said something, but she didn't quite catch it. "What?" she called over her shoulder, just before she felt a hard rap on the side of her head. Stars burst in front of her eyes, and her knees buckled beneath her.

A muffled curse met her ears as she crumpled, but she felt herself caught in midair. Unable to form a coherent word, she allowed herself to be carried upstairs. Her eyes wouldn't focus and her body felt terribly, terribly heavy. Moments—or perhaps weeks—later, she found herself lying on a bed, a cool cloth being pressed to her temple. The dark face that loomed above hers swam briefly, and then became clear. It was a scowling Tarrant Seaton, tight-jawed and intent on her wound.

"What...happened?" she whispered, her voice thready.

He didn't answer, but continued to work.

"Am I bleeding?"

His gaze flicked to meet hers. "You've got a cut, but the bleeding's stopped. I'm afraid you'll have quite a bruise."

She closed her eyes to try to ease the throbbing in her head. "Why did you hit me?"

"Hit...?" He paused, a look of disbelief on his face. "Look, I may have been tempted from time to time in the last couple of days, but I do not abuse women."

She squinted up at him. "Who did hit me, then?"

"It was a *what* that hit you. A broken beam. I tried to warn you, but you were concentrating on your notes and you ran right into it."

She grimaced, fingering the cloth that covered her temple. "What day is this, anyway? May twenty-third?"

He stared at her. "No."

She was confused. "Why do I think it's May twenty-third?"

"Maybe I'd better call a doctor," he said, sounding worried.

"Why?"

"Because it's still April second. And it's still Tuesday, no matter what your panties say."

Her face grew hot. "That's right, kick me while I'm down." Pushing herself into a sitting position, she blanched, but once upright, she discovered she was probably going to live—no dizziness, no nausea, just the awful throbbing in her head. "Give me a couple of aspirins and let's get back to work. Your mother's in a hurry for me to begin the remodeling."

He shook his head. "Not tonight. Your eye's starting to blacken."

"Oh, no," she moaned, sliding off the bed and lurching to a mirror. "Oh, no..." She watched a bluish cast begin to invade the delicate area below her eyebrow.

"I'm sorry," Tarrant offered. "No matter what our differences are, I wouldn't have wished a black eye on you."

Tentatively, she touched the tender spot.

"Did you hear me?"

She turned, supporting herself on the antique dresser. "Yes. And I accept your apology. I've never heard of you beating up on women—just their hearts."

For a fleeting instant he looked insulted. "I'll go see if your car is ready," he mumbled, leaving the room.

She chewed her lower lip. That had been uncalled-for, bringing up his well-documented power over women's hearts. It wasn't her business how he affected women. Unfortunately, today she'd been served a small taste of that effect, and it had proved all too real.

She looked back in the mirror and simply stared for several bleak minutes. Disheveled and completely drained by this ridiculous day, she watched as half her face seemed to swell. With a dismal sigh, she allowed herself an uncharacteristic lapse into self-pity. *Why me? Why in front of Tarrant Seaton, of all the men in the world?*

He was suddenly there, reflected in the mirror as he stood framed in the bedroom door. His features were solemn. "It'll be about half an hour. Your tire is resisting being patched, so Chauncey's going to put in a new tube."

Angela shook her head dejectedly, hating to be in debt to this man in any way. "Thanks," she murmured. "But I insist on paying for it."

His eyes narrowed, but apparently he decided not to argue the point. "You can deduct it from our bill if you like."

She realized she could, and that knowledge soothed her injured pride. "Don't think I won't," she promised both him and herself.

His shrug was one of complete disinterest. Doubtless the cost of an inner tube was low on the list of expenses that could topple his financial empire.

"You ought to have some ice on that eye. The cook is fixing an ice-pack and we can have some coffee while you're waiting for your car."

She nodded listlessly. What choice did she have?

Twenty minutes later, they were sitting at the big pine table in a kitchen glowing with the beauty of raised-panel cabinets and heartwood flooring. Tarrant leaned forward and frowned at her. "You're really going to have a shiner."

Holding the ice pack against her temple, she gazed down into the depths of her coffee cup and sighed. He didn't have to tell her that. Although the aspirin he'd given her was helping, every blink was painful.

"Do you think you'll be able to drive?"

"I don't know. I've never had a black eye. Do you go blind or something?"

She heard a low grunt that might have been a chuckle. "No, you don't go blind. I just thought you might be dizzy or have double vision. I should call a doctor."

She shook her head. "I'm not dizzy and I can see just fine."

"How's the coffee?" he asked after a lengthy pause.

She sipped. He was trying to make conversation, but she didn't feel like talking. "Strong," she offered, hoping he'd be satisfied with a minimal reply.

"Are you sure you're feeling all right?"

She looked up at him. "I'm not going to sue if that's what you're afraid of."

Empty minutes passed while his jaw worked spasmodically. Finally he said quietly, "Suing me is up to you. It might be a more straightforward way to try and get my money than your original plan."

Angela grew still, coffee cup poised at her lips. "What did you say?" she asked, her voice hushed with disbelief.

"You heard me." He eyed her levelly.

"Look—" she set her cup down with a thunk, sloshing coffee on the wood "—I've taken about all I intend to take from you." She stood abruptly, the ice pack falling to the floor, forgotten. "Because of your crude prank in the lunchroom, you've made my life practically unbearable at the factory. I've been baited and annoyed all afternoon about my supposed plot to trap you into marriage, and I've had it up to my—my black eye!"

He stood, too, his expression darkening. "Appropriately put. Let's just call my little *prank* an eye for an eye."

Looming over her, his broad frame seemed to take on nerve-racking dimensions. She brought herself up to her full, affronted, five-foot-five-inch height. "Oh, no! From where I stand, it doesn't look like we're so even. First, go hit yourself in the head with a rafter!"

"Don't worry, Miss Meadows. I've been punished, thanks to you." He gaze locked with hers. "What did you think would happen when your wacky mother came over to my table and announced that I was going to marry you? I have a number of associates who eat there and who heard it—one, an editor at the *Wichita Daily Press*. And in case you didn't know this, I was bombarded with calls all yesterday afternoon and this morning. That, Miss Meadows, is why our appointment was delayed.

"I, too, was baited and annoyed, as you put it. And not only by people I knew, but by newspapers. Gossip rags like *He and She* magazine, even the TV show 'Hot Topics,' gave me a call. So, you think you had a bad day? What sort of a day—two days—do you think I've had because of you and your mother?" He strode over to the kitchen counter. Leaning heavily against it, he dropped his head forward, as though he was very tired. "Don't be surprised if you're mentioned in gossip columns for a while."

"Me? I haven't done anything to be gossiped about."

His laughter was harsh. "Welcome to the real world, sweetheart."

"But... but, I—" she sputtered. "Don't try to tar me with the same dirty brush as you!"

"I don't have to. The scandal sheets will do just fine on their own. I can see the headlines now: 'Pregnant Dream Bride Left Abandoned.'"

"Pregnant!"

"By the time the story makes the rounds, you will be—probably with twins."

"Do you expect me to feel sorry for you? To believe all that trash they print is just—"

"Trash." He turned to confront her. "And now you've contributed to it." Nostrils flaring with annoyance, he drawled, "Thanks one hell of a lot."

His revelation knocked some of the bite out of her anger, but not all. Unhappy and confused, she spat, "I don't have to stand here and listen to this." When she began walking toward a door, she realized it was the entrance to the pantry. She spun around and hurried in another direction but was brought up short when she discovered she was heading back into the basement. With an exasperated groan, she cried, "What's the confounded way out of here?"

She started to backtrack and slammed directly into Tarrant's chest. The only thing that kept her from falling was his reflexive grab for her.

With the impact of their collision, she saw a white flash of light, and she would have staggered blindly and crumpled to the floor if he hadn't been holding her. Befuddled, she muttered, "May twenty-third... It *is* May twenty-third...."

In the ensuing silence the kitchen clock ticked away the seconds as she watched his features grow rigid.

"What about May twenty-third?" he asked at long last, the softness of his question at odds with the fierceness in his eyes.

Her head throbbed mercilessly, but it wasn't the dull pounding that made her shrink back. It was his stormy expression. He looked angry enough to throw her bodily across the room. Pressing her hands against his chest, she protested, "Let me go."

"What do you know about May twenty-third?" he demanded.

She blinked, not comprehending why she'd said that. "Just... let me go...."

"Why?" he asked with a slow, ironic grin. "I'm enjoying your little act. Go on, tell me about May twenty-third. Is that the day you've ordained for our wedding, by chance?" His voice was smooth, hard, unyielding. "What is the bottom line, here, Miss Meadows? Are you hoping for some sort of payoff? Will that get you off my back?"

"I don't know why I said that," she confessed, her need to be away from him as great as her sudden, strange desire to remain in his arms.

"I believe I'll hazard a guess as to why you said it, Angela, my love," he whispered, his eyes harboring a dangerous light.

"Don't bother," she squeaked, her heart racing with apprehension. Why did the mere fact that he had murmured her name make her feel weak? The reaction was absurd, insane...undeniable.

"It's no bother," he assured her, his face drawing closer. "Could it be you said it because you're a calculating little...?"

His voice had dropped to a husky register, and her heart hammered with a crazy mixture of anticipation and dread. She shook her head, denying his accusation, denying what she feared was about to happen, but neither the negative motion of her head nor the wretched whimper that escaped her throat halted him. When his mouth was a hair's breadth above hers, he said perversely, "If we're to be married, don't you think I'm entitled to kiss my bride?"

"Please..." She pushed away from him with all her might, but to no avail. She couldn't escape; his strength was far superior to hers.

As she closed her eyes, prepared to endure the contemptuous onslaught of his lips, she was startled to hear him curse. Abruptly, he let her go as though she'd become a red-hot poker.

Flustered and bewildered, she stumbled away from him. "What...? Why didn't you...?" she began, her voice faltering. Some malcontented demon deep inside her was wailing and moaning because her lips were not, right this instant, being caressed by his.

"You're wondering why I didn't kiss you, Miss Meadows?" An odd shadow flickered across his face, perhaps self-disgust, but it was gone too quickly for her to be sure. His angular features now tightly controlled, he said, "I didn't kiss you, because it wouldn't have been fair. I don't mean it wouldn't be fair to you—humbling you like that would have been all you deserved. But only a heel could do that to someone who looks as pitiful as you do right now." His lip curled in evident revulsion. "No matter what you may think, Miss Meadows, I am something of a gentleman."

She was struggling to pull her wits together, but she still felt too dazed to rebuke him, to defend herself, or to run screaming for her life. At this point she was too confused to even guess which might be the best move. She could only cower there, staring at him.

When she said nothing, impatience sparked in his eyes. "Dammit! You're the most infuriating, scheming woman I've ever met." Retreating a few steps, he raked his fingers through his perfect hair, mussing it in a most intriguing way. "I don't know how you pulled that date out of the air—and I don't care—but all your game playing won't change one inevitable fact."

She gaped at him, unable to understand his meaning.

"May the twenty-third is *my* wedding date, Miss Meadows." There was the merest pause, but time enough for his narrowed gaze to flash a distinct warning. "Mine...and Eden Leslie's."

CHAPTER FOUR

ANGELA SIDLED into the tiny kitchenette, keeping her left side turned away from her mother, though Minny was oblivious to anything but her latest hobby—making jewelry from household items. This morning, she was in the process of trimming away at a tomato can with tin snips.

"You realize you could get tetanus when that necklace rusts, don't you?" Angela warned, shaking her head at Minny.

Minny looked up from her work, scattered over the Formica top of their rickety breakfast table. "Good morning, sweetie," she chirped at her daughter's profile. "Now, you mustn't be shortsighted where creativity is concerned. Remember the Pet Rock."

Angela fished around in the refrigerator. "Well, I don't think a Pet Tetanus Necklace would have quite the same appeal."

Minny laughed, stringing another bent piece of the can onto a length of nylon fishing line. "Actually, I'm working on some ideas for my mother-of-the-bride outfit. What would you think if I made myself a hand-painted caftan to set off this piece? Oh, that reminds me, sweetie, what colors are your bridesmaids going to wear?"

With that reminder of the Seaton-marriage ordeal, Angela opted to forgo food. Her stomach had just taken a lurch for the worse. Straightening, she closed the door and edged to the coffeepot to pour herself a cup.

After a sustaining sip, she took a seat at the table, bravely displaying her damaged face for her mother to see. Giving a tired sigh, she said, "Mother, Tarrant Seaton is engaged."

Minny continued to snip irregular shapes from the can's lid. "Of course he is, sweetie. Didn't I tell him so myself?"

Reaching across the table, Angela put her hand over her mother's, halting her activity. "No, Mother. I mean he's really engaged—to someone else. That pretty blonde in The Plethora."

Minny's face puckered with uncertainty. "Where did you hear such a thing?" She looked up at her daughter and her eyes widened. "Oh, my gracious! What have I told you about eating grape-jelly sandwiches in bed?"

Angela couldn't stifle a weary smile. "Mother, I haven't done that since I was nine years old. My face is purple because it's bruised. It happened at the Seaton mansion last night."

Minny's mouth dropped open. "Did your young man strike you? Why, we'll have the law on him, that's what we'll do!" Her hands fluttered to her cheeks, and she exclaimed, "Had I known what a ruffian he was, I would never had said those nice things about him to that woman from the *National Tattler*."

Angela, who had been trying to explain that Tarrant had not beaten her, was shocked into silence by the last remark. "What—what woman from the *National Tattler*, Mother?" she finally managed, getting a very bad feeling in her stomach. She hoped it was just the effect of the reheated day-old coffee.

"Oh, she was a reporter who called to ask about my dream." Minny beamed at the memory. "She was so interested, sweetie. Why, I wouldn't be surprised if there isn't a story about us in the *Tattler* very soon. Did you know that paper goes to every grocery store in the country?''

Angela tightened her lips in chagrin. Tarrant had told her this might happen, but she hadn't thought her own mother would be a party to it. ''Mother,'' she began as calmly as she could, ''first, Tarrant Seaton didn't hit me. As a matter of fact, he helped me. Secondly, please don't talk to any more reporters about your dream. Mr. Seaton told me last night that he's engaged to that woman we saw him with in The Plethora. So that's the end of it.'' Jerking up a hand to halt her mother's protest, she went on, ''I beg you, just let this dream thing die a quiet death. Face it—it was a mistake, and now it's over.''

Minny's face grew stern. ''Daughter, I'd hate to think you doubted my powers.''

Angela heaved a woebegone sigh. ''It's not that I doubt your powers, Mother, but you have to admit you have made a few mistakes.''

Minny harrumphed. ''Name one.''

Angela cast her gaze down to the slivers of tin scattered about the table and toyed absently with her cup. ''What about the time you dreamed a frozen-food truck was going to have a terrible accident?''

Minny thought about it for a minute. ''Oh, yes. Three years ago. That was the night I had that awful frozen-fish entrée. What about it?''

''So, as we were driving down Kellogg the next day, you saw a frozen-food truck and insisted on braking immediately so we could flag it down. Remember?''

Minny nodded. ''Certainly. And it did have an accident. I was right.''

''Yes. You were right,'' Angela echoed tiredly. ''But Mother, that truck rear-ended *our* car! Can't you see it wouldn't have had the accident if we hadn't stopped?''

Minny wagged a warning finger at her daughter. "What makes you think that truck wouldn't have had a really terrible accident somewhere down the road if it hadn't been held up where we stopped it?"

"Well, of course, I can't say that—for sure," Angela admitted reluctantly.

Minny's face brightened with a satisfied smirk. "I believe I've made my point."

Angela gave up and took a long drink of her bitter coffee. She decided not to remind her mother that the accident had been their fault, that their car had been totaled, or that they'd had to pay for the trucker's grillwork, as well as his chiropractor's bills.

"Don't worry about this so-called engagement to that blond woman, Angela," Minny offered amiably as she went back to her snipping. "Trust your mother. Oh—" she looked back up, her smile intact "—would you mind getting the paper? I think I heard Carl's truck go by."

Angela nodded without interest. "Sure."

Minutes later, Angela was staring at the *Wichita Daily Press*'s gossip column, "Famous Folks." Its purpose was to keep locals informed about the private tribulations of people in the national spotlight. Not only was there a newspaper file photo of Tarrant Seaton in all his debonair elegance, but there was one of her—the one that had been taken when she'd accepted her WSU Entrepreneur award. Unfortunately, she'd had a tooth filled that morning, and her smile hadn't been quite straight. As she stared at their pictures, her stomach did a flip-flop. Minny couldn't have conjured up a more mismatched pair if she'd dreamed through the entire Ice Age!

Tarrant was known to be dashing, well-bred, wealthy and worldly. Angela was, as the article pointed out, "a failed hog farmer's daughter." What it didn't say was that she had a mix-and-match wardrobe of marginal quality, and that a trip to Oklahoma City last summer had been her biggest claim to worldliness so far. And that had been to visit a sick aunt.

As a matter of fact, it was on that fateful trip she'd picked up a dozen pairs of panties at a factory overrun sale—all the panties had said "Wednesday." She closed her eyes, recalling the embarrassment of yesterday's disaster in Tarrant Seaton's office. She hadn't thought things could get worse, but when she opened her eyes again, there they were—still side by side in the newspaper—the Prince of Delights and Hogetta Hayseed!

Though the newspaper hadn't called her names, that was how Angela saw herself when compared to Tarrant Seaton. The headline read, "Engaged in her Dreams," and gave a tongue-in-cheek account of the purported engagement between Tarrant and herself. If anyone held any doubts that she was a money-grubbing bimbo before, the evidence presented here would erase them. But could she really blame the reporter who'd actually heard her mother's announcement? It sounded like a sleazy scam even to her!

"Oh, Mother," she groaned, handing Minny the paper. "I wonder how in the world they got this?"

The older woman studied the pictures for a minute, smiling broadly. "What a cute couple you make." She looked over at her stricken daughter. "It mentions me, too!"

"Mother," Angela repeated, her voice weak, "do you have any idea how they got my picture?"

Minny seemed exceedingly pleased with herself. "Well, naturally, I gave it to the young man who came by the apartment yesterday. He was charming. Those newspaper people are so sweet."

Angela balled her fists in her lap, appalled and furious that Minny had so little sense! "Mother! How could you do such a thing to me?" she protested. "This is terrible! What will people think?"

Minny's face fell. "Why, daughter, I do believe you have missed the point here." She spread her arms. "Tarrant Seaton's marriage is big news. You should be proud."

Angela felt ill. She knew her mother could never be convinced that what she'd done hadn't been in her daughter's best interest. In some innocent, childlike corner of her brain, Minny always managed to cling to the bright side of a calamity, no matter how obscure or downright nonexistent that bright side was. Despondent, her fruitless anger fading, Angela pleaded, "Mother, please don't talk to any more newspaper people, and *don't* give them any more pictures."

"But what would you have me say if they call? I won't be rude, Angela. I simply won't."

"Just—" Angela shook her head in mortification "—just tell them your lawyer told you not to speak to anyone."

"But we don't have a lawyer."

Feeling beaten down, Angela buried her face in her hands, flinching at the pain when she touched the bruised eye. "If you keep dreaming," she groaned, "we may be forced to retain one."

The morning was much more pleasant than she expected, considering the way it had begun. Leaving Richard in charge of the store, she'd hurried back out to Havenhearth to finish touring the storage areas and was escorted, this time, by Alexander. She'd tried to camouflage her injury by wearing an old sailor-type hat with its brim turned down. She'd tied a long scrap from one of her mother's tie-dye experiments around the brim. It matched, more or less, her navy-and-white-striped dress. Sunglasses had helped a lot. But none of her precautions had really mattered. Alexander, obviously accustomed to minding his own business, didn't even blink when she'd removed her sunglasses to see in the relative darkness of the mansion's extensive attics.

She'd been bounding down the wide front steps of Havenhearth precisely at noon, bent on getting back to her store to relieve Richard, when the ominous roar of a Lambourghini engine assaulted her ears. She quickened her pace toward her car. She was so embarrassed about last night she couldn't bear to face him.

As she tugged her car door open, a gust of wind invaded her skirt and carried the hem up to brush her chin. She dropped her briefcase and pressed the fullness down. But with only two arms to corral the billowing fabric, her success was marginal.

"Well, well," she heard a deep, amused voice remark behind her. "A flash of déjà vu."

Stiffening with resentment, she sprung to remove her backside from his view, snagging up her briefcase in the process. She tossed the case into the front seat of her car and was about to follow it in, deciding not to dignify his remark with a response, when her hat flew off.

Tarrant snagged it with surprising grace for a man of his size, and was about to hand it back when he caught a glimpse of her battered face. His teasing smile faded.

"Good Lord! That looks worse than I remember. How are you feeling?"

She was startled by his unexpected concern and didn't know how to react. The last thing Angela wanted was this man's sympathy. Still, she didn't think his remark merited the unfriendly exit she'd been about to execute. Gingerly replacing her hat so that it partially masked her injury, she murmured, "It doesn't hurt that much."

Apparently unconvinced, he said, "Right. Do I look like a fool?"

She had glanced away, but turned back, suggesting coolly, "Do yourself a favor and don't ask loaded questions."

When she was about to escape into the car, he said, "I imagine you saw the *Press* this morning."

She nodded, forcing herself to meet his suddenly guarded gaze.

"Was the coverage everything you hoped it would be?" he asked.

Smarting at the suggestion that she and her mother actually wanted such unsavory publicity, she protested, "I didn't have anything to do with that!"

"Sure," he chided with a malicious grin. "That would explain one thing, anyway."

Eyeing him resentfully and angry that she had to ask, she demanded, "What would it explain?"

"Why they used a photo that made you look like you'd been inhaling toxic fumes. No doubt the gossip-column thieves had to break in and grab it under cover of darkness, so they weren't able to see how bad a picture it was. The lengths those people go for a story."

He made a tsking sound. Sarcasm. How she loathed it. And Tarrant Seaton seemed to be better at it than any man alive! Heaving a groan of blasphemous proportions, Angela sputtered, "I... If you must know, my mother gave the reporter that picture. Mom's a little naive about some things. I told her not to talk to any more reporters. She promised she wouldn't."

He lifted a reproachful brow. "It's cowardly to blame your mother. No one who's ever met her would believe she could mastermind such a convoluted scheme."

A shaft of dismay shot through her, followed immediately by righteous fury. "Oh...you're impossible! You wouldn't believe me if I took a blood oath!" Sliding into her car, she tugged the door shut, but it wouldn't quite close. Opening it wide, she tried again, but it remained obstinately ajar.

Thoroughly frustrated, she muttered a harsh word, then found herself flushed with embarrassment. She hated the fact that Tarrant Seaton could make her so angry and then just stand there relishing her defeat.

She heard the precise clip of his footsteps as he approached, heard her door open and heard it slam shut. It stunned her that he'd bothered to close her door for her. He'd probably done it to get her to leave, she rationalized. Agitated beyond words, she dug out her car keys, fumbled to insert them and, barely short of flooding the engine, brought the old car shuddering to life. The thing rattled and protested, backfiring twice before she could get adequate power to escape down the drive.

As she pulled away, she could hear him shout after her, "You're welcome, Miss Meadows. It was my pleasure."

Angela forced herself to ignore him, to disregard his parting gibe and the nagging feeling that this time *she* had been the insensitive snob.

A week passed with embarrassing problems on the Seaton-Meadows Dream-Wedding gossip front. Not only had the *National Tattler* printed a degrading article, but she'd gotten a less-than-flattering mention in both *He and She* magazine and a national syndicated television-news show called "Hot Topics."

Angela had been mortified, having to make frequent trips to the factory and endure teasing remarks from employees—especially Marty Rainwater. Apparently the woman had an unrealistic crush on her boss and didn't like the idea of nationally publicized competition.

Luckily, Angela hadn't had to face Tarrant again. The scuttlebutt was that he'd been called away to work out a problem at his Detroit plant. That was just peachy with Angela—although it was her private opinion that he was really basking in the sun at some exclusive tropical resort. She didn't believe that Tarrant Seaton could actually work out any problem concerning any plant—even if it merely involved watering the green, leafy kind. Not the pretty-boy figurehead she knew and loathed!

Angela hadn't seen Delila, either. Maybe Delila had decided she didn't want to be around such a "mercenary, publicity-seeking gold digger," as she'd heard herself called by the terminally catty among Delila's Delights employees. At the mansion, Angela had either been left to take her measurements alone or in the nonjudgmental company of Alexander, whom she'd grown to like.

However, business had been booming at the store. Or at least, there were a lot of browsers. It seemed that notoriety bred not only contempt but some business. Surprisingly, she'd gotten a couple of new clients for custom work out of the fiasco. She wasn't happy about the way she'd gotten them. She only hoped that when this whole thing blew over, she'd earn a reputation by her good work, not her infamous past.

Today, although the store was bustling, it looked as if things were about to go downhill fast. Delila had called, asking Angela to join "us" for dinner; afterward, they would discuss the contractors who were bidding on the job. Angela hoped "us" meant that she and Delila would share a casual dinner discussing contractors with Alexander and a few of the servants, or maybe even a table-trained house cat with an interest in closet space. Any "us" would be preferable to the "us" Angela feared—Delila and her son. Angela, recognizing a direct order when she heard one, however pleasantly phrased, had accepted. All day she'd looked forward to the hour of seven o'clock with abject dread.

As her car sputtered and coughed along Havenhearth's meandering drive, that awful hour was upon her. Parking her junker, she noted with a heavy heart that there were no other cars there. Tarrant might still be in Detroit—or sunbathing on some far-flung sun-drenched beach. Unfortunately, he could also be in the mansion, his car parked in one of the garages that stretched along the west wing of the house.

As Angela reached the door, it opened, and Alexander greeted her with his usual officious scowl, which no longer intimidated her. She smiled up at him and handed him her cardigan. "Am I early?" she asked.

"No, madam." He draped her sweater over his arm and directed her to the library. "May I get you anything, Miss Meadows?"

She shook her head.

"Very well. I will tell Mrs. Seaton that you have arrived." As the last word was uttered, the doors closed between them. Angela wondered how he could time that so perfectly, then decided they probably taught Sentence Finishing While Door Closing in butler school somewhere—somewhere far from Kansas, she concluded with a wry grin.

"Ah, she smiles."

The deep voice that seemed to come out of nowhere made her jump. Spinning in a circle, she demanded breathlessly, "Where are you?"

Tarrant emerged from a high-backed chair in a shadowy corner of the room. "I didn't mean to frighten you. I assumed you saw me."

"Well, I didn't." She looked him up and down, deciding the dark gray trousers and matching pullover accentuated his allure to a point that was criminal. "When did you get back from ... wherever?"

Slipping his hands into his pockets with easy nonchalance, he gave her the same direct once-over that she'd just given him. "This afternoon. I understand you're having dinner with us."

She had an urge to smooth her skirt, positive that it was bunched up around her knees with static cling. She resisted. "I, uh, yes. But you needn't stay. Your mother and I can handle everything."

His expression held perverse amusement as he sauntered toward her. "You mean, of course, that I don't need to trouble my pretty little head with nasty business talk?"

She didn't realize her low opinion of him showed. "Don't be silly," she lied.

He laughed, drawing too close for comfort. "Don't worry about me, Miss Meadows, I'll try to keep up. Would you like a drink?"

He indicated a tray filled with bottles.

"No. I don't drink."

As he headed for the liquor cart, Angela noted how tanned he was. He must have been lounging on the beach. You couldn't get a tan like that in an office in Detroit.

"Miss Meadows?" he queried. "Did you hear me?"

"Pardon?" she asked rather brusquely, wondering what her turn of mind had caused her to miss.

"I asked if you'd like a glass of orange juice. I'm having tomato juice myself."

She shook her head.

He poured himself a glass of juice and suggested, "You might as well sit down. Mother is always late."

Angela took a seat on the couch, allowing herself a long, despondent sigh. She hoped, just this once, that the fates would take pity on her, and Delila would appear quickly. She didn't like being here alone with this disturbing man.

It surprised her when Tarrant joined her on the couch, since there were perfectly good places to sit farther away. Though she hadn't wanted anything, he handed her a glass of tomato juice. There was a spring of celery lolling in it, giving the drink an incongruous Christmassy feel.

She took it and murmured a halfhearted thank-you.

"Since we can't seem to agree on anything, I suppose you hate tomato juice," he remarked after he'd taken a sip.

"No, it's not that. It's just that I...my stomach...I'm not very hungry."

Removing the glass from her hand, he put it on the tray table in front of them. "Would you like some soda and bitters? Sometimes that helps settle the stomach."

He was up before she could insist he not bother. And he had the drink mixed and poured and was back before she could even begin to marvel at his behavior. He was certainly playing the role of good host to the hilt.

"Thank you," she muttered, trying the drink. It tasted strange, but did seem to help.

"I see your eye is better," he remarked, picking up his juice again.

She nodded, sipping, keeping her gaze on the rim of her glass.

"I also see that the fuss about our alleged wedding has died down."

She choked, but got control of herself. "Yes."

"How did you like being a celebrity for a week?"

She slanted him a cheerless look. "Not much."

He chuckled dryly. "I know the feeling."

When her drink was half-finished, she put it on the table. Since he'd opened the subject, she decided to ask him something that had been bothering her all week. "How did Eden take all this?"

He had just placed his glass beside hers. At her question he paused, his expression softening at the mention of his fiancée. "She took it extremely well. But then, Eden is quite a woman."

For some reason, Angela felt a twinge of distress, though she couldn't fathom the reason. Why would it upset her to know that Tarrant Seaton had nothing but good things to say about the woman he loved? Placing her hands in her lap and clenching them tightly, she declared, "You're a lucky man."

He smiled, and that lone dimple in his left cheek sent an unwanted thrill up her spine. "People make their own luck, Miss Meadows. I hope you won't be offended if I tell you that you have enough brains and gumption to be successful on your own. You don't have to catch a man to get what you want."

Angela's expression clouded, and she found herself caught between feeling offended and feeling flattered. First of all, she *knew* she could make it on her own—had always planned to make it on her own. Secondly, she'd never had any intention of *catching* any man! When the jumble of her emotions settled, she found herself more annoyed than flattered.

Pride forced her to stand as she retorted, "I *am* offended. But I will say this, Mr. Seaton—I'm tickled pink that you've found a woman who's willing to take you on, because I, for one, wouldn't have you for all the ..."

"Money in the world?" he finished for her, a cynical edge to his voice.

She was seething, her temper rolling over her good sense. She'd had all the sarcasm, humiliation and patronizing she could stand! Unable to find words stinging enough, she swung out blindly with her hand.

As he grabbed her wrist, he shot to his feet, suddenly towering over her, his face set in stern lines.

She yanked, but it did no good. "Let go!"

"Dammit, woman," he growled. "Can't we spend five minutes together without one of us blowing sky-high? I was trying to compliment you."

"Oh!" she wailed. "If that's your idea of a compliment ..."

All the things that had happened to her since she'd met this man came back in a raging flood—every taunt, jeer and put-down of the past week. It was suddenly just too much! With a strangled cry, she lashed out at him with her left hand and found it caught as securely as her right.

Obviously trying to gain better control over the woman who'd turned into a wildcat, Tarrant forced her arms around to her back until she was straining against him. His grip wasn't painful, but that didn't matter to Angela in her frustration and fury. She struggled, calling out, "You bully! Let me go!"

She'd been about to stomp on his foot, but he thwarted her by shifting his weight and making her lose her balance. In the process, he had to pull her closer to keep her from falling.

Sudden tears blurred her vision. "Let go of me!" she pleaded, wanting to get away. She was so confused, so unhappy. "Don't touch me!"

"That would be my pleasure," he declared with savage harshness. "But if you'll recall, you were trying to slap me."

"Well, you've been so mean to me. You drove me—"

"Drove *you!* If you want the truth, you're driving me—" He broke off roughly. When he abruptly let her go, she stumbled backward, trembling, her breathing ragged.

By the time she'd gathered enough poise to meet his gaze, his expression had returned to one of indifference, except for a slight tenseness around the mouth. "Perhaps you're right, Miss Meadows," he stated evenly. "I think I'll leave you and Mother to have your business dinner alone."

Without another word, he headed away from her, and it dismayed Angela to realize the ease with which he could dismiss what had just happened. Her humiliation had clearly meant nothing to him! Not a whisper of an apology, not a syllable of remorse for his brutish actions! She wondered if Eden was aware that she was getting an unfeeling beast for a husband.

Just as he reached the door, it opened, and Delila Seaton appeared, looking elegant in draped green silk. "Hello, Tarrant. Hello, Angela, I—"

"Why, here you are at last, Mother," Tarrant interrupted smoothly, giving her a kiss on the cheek. "I won't be staying for dinner, after all. I've just remembered a pressing engagement in Wichita. Besides, Miss Meadows and I had a long talk, and we're both quite clear on...everything."

Delila's smile faded slightly. "Oh? All right, dear...."

With a casual arm, he encircled her shoulders. "By the way, Mother, you must try to be on time in the future. I'm afraid I wasn't very entertaining company for Miss Meadows."

Squeezing his mother's shoulders, he addressed Angela. "You'll never know how much I enjoyed seeing you again, Miss Meadows." His dark eyes glinted like cold steel, making his real message abundantly clear. Angela could leap off a cliff for all he cared!

She swallowed. Her throat had gone dry as dust.

He turned away and was gone, leaving Delila looking confused. She shook her head. "Goodness. He's in a rare mood." When she faced Angela, her expression changed to one of concern. "You look pale, dear. I hope Tarrant didn't upset you. It's that assertive nature of his. Some people are intimidated by it, but he truly doesn't mean to be unkind."

Angela surreptitiously wiped away a tear, muttering under her breath, "That's a joke."

"Forgive me, I didn't hear you," Delila said as she moved toward her guest.

"Er, perfect *host*," Angela fabricated, her voice weak. "Mr. Seaton is always the perfect host." Feeling peculiarly trembly in the legs, she lowered herself to the couch.

CHAPTER FIVE

THE NEXT DAY, Angela strolled about her colorful shop, paying scant attention to the browsers as her thoughts insisted on wandering back to Tarrant Seaton and the calamitous events of the evening before.

She fingered one of the wire baskets that could be stacked to go under kitchen counters or as extra shelves in closets, wishing she hadn't blown up the way she had. How unprofessional! Tarrant had been trying to be nice, after all. What was it about him that made her so touchy?

She walked absentmindedly toward the back of her small, jam-packed shop, where the watertight, bright-hued plastic storage containers were aligned in rows. Without much interest, she noted that the large blue under-the-bed storage cartons were getting low, and made a mental note to reorder.

"Excuse me, miss?"

Angela was roused from her thoughts by a jeans-clad woman dragging a wailing preschooler. "Excuse me, miss?" she repeated, almost shouting over the shrieking child. "Where are your wire shelf makers? You know, the long mesh shelves with four legs that stack to make extra closet shelves?"

Forcing Tarrant's face from her mind, she offered the child one of the lollipops she kept in her jacket pocket for such occasions. "The Stretched Stackables are on special this week. They're up front beside the cash register." With a polite smile, she added, "The young man in the red vest will be happy to help you."

The woman threw a harried glance over her shoulder, then, spotting the display, smiled bashfully. "Oh, for Pete's sake." She met Angela's gaze and nodded her thanks. "I walked right past them. I feel so stupid."

Even in her unhappy state of mind, Angela had to laugh. "You're not alone. There are lots of days when I feel like the reigning queen of stupid," she replied honestly.

With a giggle, the young mother hurried toward the front; her child, quiet now, licked her candy. As Angela turned back, she saw Minny enter from the rear, her voluminous jumpsuit billowing in her wake.

"Hello, Mother," Angela said. "Something smells good. What are you cooking up there?"

Minny waved a refuting hand. "I'm not cooking, sweetie. I'm experimenting with a special glaze. I just dipped some dog biscuits in it and I'm drying them in the oven."

Angela grimaced. "Why in heaven's name are you glazing dog biscuits?"

Minny grinned impishly. "Why, I'm creating earrings, sweetie. Can't you see it? Dog-biscuit earrings. They'll be all the rage one day. Mark my words!"

Angela wasn't even going to ask what went into the glaze, but she did say, "Mother, I hope your glaze is environmentally safe."

Minny snickered. "Of course it is, sweetie. As a matter of fact, we're having the leftover glaze as a sauce on our broccoli at dinner."

Angela's eyes widened, but before she could question her mother about the wisdom of such an idea, Minny whispered excitedly, "My goodness! I do believe that customer who just came in is Delila of Delila's Delights herself. You didn't tell me she was coming by, sweetie. Do invite her to stay for dinner!''

Angela tried to hide her horror at the idea of Delila Seaton consuming dog-biscuit varnish at *her* invitation. She patted her mother's arm as much in appeasement as affection. ''I'm sure Mrs. Seaton is busy, Mother—''

''Pish tosh!'' Minny declared, undaunted. ''We really should get to know each other, since you and dear Tarrant are going to be married.''

The last was stated as Minny bustled toward the front of the store and Delila Seaton. It took Angela a moment to shake off her shock, so she was a bit tardy reaching Delila. Minny was already proposing dinner and stating the reason they must get to know each other better—which was that they would ''soon be related by marriage.''

Angela felt her blood seep out of her toes as Delila gazed down at Minny, the shorter of the two. ''Why, Mrs. Meadows,'' she purred in that husky voice, ''you are very kind to want to include me in your dinner plans. It does smell wonderful.''

''Thank you.'' Minny beamed. ''But that's my dog bis—''

''Mrs. Seaton,'' Angela interrupted, stepping between the women, hoping to save her mother from yet again being labeled nutty. ''I assume you've come to choose the wooden modules for the pantry and master bedroom?''

Delila shifted her gaze from Minny to Angela and then back to Minny. ''Dog bis?'' she asked.

''Dog-biscuit glaze. I'm creating a new craze in earrings,'' Minny revealed proudly. ''You know, Delila, you're not the only savvy businesswoman in town. There's me—'' she swept an expansive arm toward Angela ''—and my baby, of course.''

Delila's expression softened from the frown of confusion to mild merriment. "I can see that. Dog-biscuit earrings. Who would have thought...?"

Angela winced at what Delila must be thinking. "Mother," she broke in, "Mrs. Seaton told me she only had half an hour to devote to our project this afternoon. Maybe you could discuss your jewelry creations some other time."

"Yes," Delila agreed. "I know, why don't you and Angela join me this Saturday evening for dinner, Mrs. Meadows? I'd love to discuss your jewelry then."

Minny clasped her fluttery hands together. "Why, I'd be delighted, Delila. I'll even make you a gift of a pair of my newest design."

Angela had a mental flash of Delila Seaton garbed in elegant evening wear, with a pair of dog biscuits dangling from her ears. Improbable to say the least!

"How kind of you to offer," Delila said graciously, "but I can accept them only if you take a box of my chocolate-covered strawberries in return."

"Oh, rapture!" Minny exclaimed. "I assure you I shall be getting the better deal. They're heaven on earth."

"Why, thank you, Minny. I may just use that phrase in my advertising."

To Angela's astonishment, Delila's remark seemed completely sincere.

Turning from Minny, Delila said, "And now, we'd probably better get to work, Angela dear."

"Goodbye Delila," Minny called. "I must go stir the sauce for the broccoli. It could very well become as hard as a wisdom tooth if I don't."

When she'd scurried away, Delila gave Angela a confused look. "What kind of sauce gets that hard?"

Angela smiled wearily. "Just Mother's."

Delila laughed, seeming pleasantly surprised. "How could a solid, down-to-earth young woman such as yourself have such a charmingly impractical mother?"

Angela plunged her hands into her jacket pockets and shrugged. "It was her charming impracticality that made me what I am. Somebody had to be practical, or the world would have come crashing down on us years ago." She turned to consider Delila, who was watching her intently. "But don't think I'm not proud of her. She helped me get where I am," Angela finished, her tone vaguely defensive.

Delila smiled kindly. "I'm sure she helped you a great deal. You have every right to be proud of her."

Angela felt as though Delila really meant it, and that, for some odd reason, the elegant woman had taken an instant liking to Minny. She hadn't thought that possible. She'd thought Delila would have no patience for Minny—have an attitude more like Tarrant's. She was glad she'd been wrong.

With a wave of her hand she directed Delila to the narrow room that was partitioned off from the main store. This was where the more expensive wooden modules were displayed in styles ranging from Country French to Danish Modern. Here was where custom buyers were shown catalogs full of the well-designed storage arrangements available to them. Delila Seaton was interested in only the best, and though Angela had offered to take the catalogs to Delila's home—no small feat—Delila had insisted on coming down to the store. Angela blessed her for her thoughtfulness.

They seated themselves at a catalog-strewn table that stood amid polished samples of cherry, oak and pine shelving of all sizes, as well as an endless variety of square modules. All the styles could be fitted together in myriad ways.

Angela was withdrawing her preliminary sketches from her briefcase when Delila touched her hand, stilling her movement. Angela glanced curiously at the older woman. When their eyes met, Delila asked, ''Are you fond of my son, Angela?''

She was taken aback by the unexpected question. ''Why, I, uh, we really don't know each other very well,'' she managed at last. She could never tell this woman what she really thought of her son—that he was cold, unfeeling and cynical.

Delila's expression had grown vaguely uneasy. ''I try to stay out of my son's business, dear, but I would have to be quite a fool not to notice the publicity about you and Tarrant and a predicted marriage.''

Angela tensed. ''I'm very sorry about that, Mrs. Seaton. I assure you, it's all been a terrible misunderstanding.''

Delila continued to watch Angela for a minute before she spoke. ''Well, when your mother mentioned that she thought you and Tarrant—''

''Mother has these...dreams,'' Angela explained hurriedly, shaking her head. ''She's convinced that Mr. Seaton and I... Oh, don't worry. I have no conniving notions in that direction. I swear. I've tried to explain to Mr. Seaton that my mother, though she means well, has made a dreadful mistake. I'm sorry I can't convince him of that, but I promise you, Mother means no harm.''

''I see.'' The corners of Delila's mouth lifted wryly. ''Well, she certainly is one of a kind.''

Angela's expression softened. ''That's true.''

''I'll look forward to seeing you both on Saturday, then?''

Angela nodded as she drew out her sketchbook. Personally, she dreaded the thought of having dinner at Havenhearth.

"By the way, Eden Leslie will be there," Delila added as she slipped a pair of reading glasses from her brocade bag.

Angela didn't say anything. Was this a subtle warning? No doubt. She only hoped she could convince her mother not to give Eden any further condolences over losing Tarrant!

She mentally counted the things she would have to contend with next Saturday night—dog-biscuit earrings, Eden Leslie's proprietary presence, Tarrant Seaton's taunting gaze. All in all, the possibilities didn't bode well for a placid evening.

As ANGELA'S CAR ka-chugged along the winding drive toward Havenhearth, she decided she'd better remind her mother once more about what she was *not* to talk about. "Remember, Mother, please don't mention any weddings. Eden Leslie and Tarrant Seaton will be married on the twenty-third of next month, and that's that."

Minny, who'd been fiddling with the pink ribbon on her little gift box, turned toward her daughter. "May twenty-third? How in heaven's name do you know that? There's been nothing official in the papers."

Angela suddenly wished she'd kept her mouth shut. She'd never told her mother about her wretched encounter with Tarrant the night she'd banged her head. She curled her fingers more tightly around the steering wheel and decided not to answer at all.

"Did Tarrant tell you? Did Delila? Are you absolutely sure about this? I think you're wrong. I still think—"

"Oh, Mother, for goodness' sake. I'm sure. Tarrant told me."

"When?" Minny had shifted in her seat and was wide-eyed and scowling at the same time, as though she was going to fight this tooth and nail. "I don't believe it. What about my dream? Have you no faith in me, sweetie? Don't you believe in my power?"

"Mother," Angela said through a weary sigh. "It's just that, well, I hit my head. You know, when I got that black eye. And for some stupid reason, I thought it was May twenty-third when I came to. Tarrant became very distressed and decided I was predicting the date for his marriage to me. I mean, with all the publicity, he was naturally suspicious of me. So..." Angela braked the car in front of the mansion and turned off the engine before she faced her mother with the news. "He told me in no uncertain terms that he was getting married on that day but it wasn't to me, it was to Eden Leslie." She reached over and touched her mother's knee, or what she thought might be a knee beneath all that tie-dyed muslin. "That's why I want you to just keep a lid on the whole subject. Please?"

Minny was frowning, apparently deep in thought.

"Mother?" Angela shook Minny's knee, trying to draw her from her strange stupor.

With a suddenness that made Angela jump, Minny cried, "That's it! Of course! Why didn't you tell me of your vision before, sweetie? This confirms it. You will marry Tarrant Seaton, and it will be on May twenty-third as you prophesied."

Angela was aghast. "I prophesied no such thing!"

Minny was smiling broadly now. "Sweetie, don't you see it? I didn't have the power to dream the future until I met your father. You now have the same power, since you've met *your* true love." A look of pure bliss brightening her face, she clasped the gift between her hands, not noticing she was crushing the bow.

Angela was about to caution her mother not to go over-board when the car door was pulled open. She whirled around, startled. "Oh," she breathed. "Hello, Chauncey. I didn't see you."

Chauncey, the Seaton chauffeur, was standing there, tall and terribly imposing in his gray uniform. He smiled, or at least he seemed to, for his salt-and-pepper mustache twitched. "Madam. It's nice to see you. And I'm sure you know I've grown quite fond of your automobile."

She appreciated his droll wit and made an effort to smile. "We'll try not to flatten any tires this evening when we shut the doors."

"Allow me to close the doors." His mustache twitched again. "However, serving you in any way is my pleasure, madam."

Minny leaned across her daughter and waved. "Hello, I'm madam's mother, Minny. You look like a man who'd want a pair of dog-biscuit earrings for your wife. What do you say? Half price, today only."

Chauncey's bushy brows drew together in confusion. "I beg your pardon?"

Angela scrambled out of the driver's seat. "Never mind, Chauncey. Come on, Mother. We'll be late if we dawdle."

Chauncey stepped back and removed his hat, watching with subdued astonishment as Minny scrambled across the seat and all but fell out. Trying to straighten the fabric flapping in the breeze about her, she twittered, "My door's jammed, and I don't crawl out as well as I once did. Makes a mess of my accoutrements. I design my own, you know."

Chauncey's mustache twitched yet again. "And they suit you, madam," he remarked in his reserved way.

Minny beamed. "Why, how sweet! Just for that, I'll send you a complimentary pair of my dog-biscuit earrings. I'd give you mine, but then what would I wear in my ears?''

"I wouldn't know, madam," Chauncey responded benignly. "Perhaps . . . hubcaps?''

"Chauncey," Angela cautioned, "don't help.''

This time, Chauncey's shoulders quivered, and Angela shook her head at him, but she couldn't be angry. Chauncey was such a nice man with a keen sense of the ridiculous. It was odd that the Seaton mansion seemed to be full of good-humored people. She wondered why none of it had rubbed off on Tarrant.

Hurriedly, she led her mother toward the door as the older woman embarked on a rambling recital about the possibilities of abandoned hubcaps as potential fashion statements.

Angela tried not to shudder. The evening was off to a rocky start.

Upon entering the mansion, they were led to the library by the ever-austere Alexander. Angela was uncomfortable in the library, where Tarrant had so rudely held her captive in his arms and then tossed her aside like yesterday's *Wall Street Journal.*

Lamentably, the first person she spied was the rude master of the mansion. Tarrant stood before the marble fireplace, tall and splendid-looking in a green silk blazer and rust-colored slacks. His black hair, infernally perfect, set off the deep tan of his face and enhanced the duskiness of his eyes. He was not quite smiling, but he seemed pleasantly disposed. Perhaps that was because at his right stood the willowy Eden Leslie, draped in mauve faille that clung to her lithe body. She seemed like some elegant image that had stepped out of a high-fashion magazine and into real life. Her blond hair was swept back from a sweet, ivory-pale face and hung in a regal French braid to just below her shoulder blades. Tarrant and Eden seemed the perfect socially elite couple, and for some stupid reason, that didn't sit as well with Angela as it should have.

She self-consciously smoothed her skirt—neither designer nor floor-length. Why, oh why, didn't she have a floor-length dress? *Because,* her practical side retorted, *you don't have the money for such frivolous luxuries.*

As was her habit, or her shortcoming, Delila was not in attendance. Minny, unbothered by social peculiarities, promenaded across the room to where Eden and Tarrant were standing and put out her hand. "Hello there, son. How are you doing? My, you're looking handsomer than ever!" She shook Tarrant's hand with both of hers, disregarding the fact that he hadn't offered it.

While one hand was being pumped, Tarrant gestured toward Eden and said, "Mrs. Meadows, this is my fiancée, Eden Leslie—"

"Uh-uh," Minny cautioned with a wag of her finger. "We aren't talking about that this evening. I promised Angela." Releasing Tarrant from her grasp, she picked up the blond woman's hand and began to pump anew. "It's so nice to meet you, Eden. Call me Minny." Looking over her shoulder at Angela, who was beating a hasty path toward them, Minny added in a clandestine whisper, "No hard feelings, I hope?"

A confused expression crossed Eden's face. "About what, Mrs. . . . Minny?"

Minny winked. "About the you-know-what on May twenty-third. But you're a pretty thing. You'll find somebody else."

When she finally reached them, Angela didn't know quite what Minny had said. But judging by the narrowing of Tarrant's gaze, she was fairly sure they weren't discussing the current humid spell. "Er, how do you do." Angela extended her own hand toward Eden, hoping her mother would take the hint and let go of Eden's. It worked.

Eden clasped Angela's hand and smiled good-naturedly. "It's nice to finally meet you," she offered in a voice that surprised Angela. It wasn't as honeyed as she'd thought it would be, but held an unsophisticated twang, instead.

Eden's gentle blue eyes compelled Angela to blurt, "I'm so sorry about all that awful publicity. I hope you weren't upset by it."

Eden shook her head. "Tarrant explained it all to me. I understand." She laughed gaily, adding, "I suppose a woman who's engaged to a man like Tarrant must expect a certain amount of competition."

"But I'm not—"

"Forgive me," Eden interrupted. "I didn't mean you." She patted Angela's arm. "Let's just forget it."

Angela smiled faintly. "You're very gracious."

"Yes, she is," Tarrant agreed, drawing Angela's reluctant gaze. He was regarding her with half-closed eyes—no doubt comparing her unfavorably with Eden. Her blue-and-white-checked gingham dress was a far cry from the elegance of Eden's outfit.

"You look very nice tonight," he remarked quietly, surprising Angela. "As do you, Minny."

Angela could only stare at him. Had she misread his intense appraisal? Was he being sarcastic? His voice hadn't seemed to carry a derogatory tone....

Unlike Angela, Minny was not stilled into shock by his compliment. She giggled. "You're so sweet, son. It's my own creation. Now be truthful—how do you like my earrings?"

He appeared to study them for a moment before he actually grinned and said, "They're absolutely you, Minny."

His tone was so unexpectedly friendly, Angela was startled. What was with him? Apparently he planned to be on his most gentlemanly behavior tonight. For Eden's benefit? Well, whatever the reason, it was the best news she'd had all week.

"Oh, son, you're such a tease," Minny was saying. "I've brought a pair of my doggy-biscuit earrings for your mother, you know. I do hope she'll be here."

"She will," Tarrant assured her as he twined his fingers with Eden's. "She has a tendency to be late."

Angela glanced from his dark hand, holding Eden's smaller, paler one, to his face. A certain tension in his voice had seemed to suggest he was recalling the last time Delila had been late to dinner. When her eyes met his, Tarrant averted his gaze. But she could tell he'd been watching her.

She was uncomfortable. Tarrant was holding his fiancée's hand but his fleeting glance had seemed almost guilty. And she, too, felt a strange culpability. That was absurd, of course. Nothing at all had happened between them. Nevertheless the feeling nagged at her.

Even an hour later, when they were finishing dinner, Angela felt the same odd sense of having been involved in an indiscretion with Tarrant. And the occasional sober glances he'd slanted her way hadn't helped.

During the meal, Angela had found out a number of things about Eden. She'd been divorced for two years, and her father had managed several of the Seaton properties. Eden had been very close to Tarrant while they were growing up. At eighteen she'd met and married a wealthy Texas rancher. That was twelve years ago. And though it hadn't been stated openly, Angela got the feeling that Eden's ex-husband had had an affair, ending the marriage.

It was obvious that Tarrant and Eden were fond of each other. Angela toyed with her food, wishing she could be happier about that fact. And just why she wasn't evaded her completely.

The evening had been filled with laughter and bright conversation. Angela had even managed to join in a time or two, though her gloomy mood continued to pester her. It was after nine when a smartly clad kitchen maid brought out a large dish and then, with a flourish, set it on fire.

Angela gasped in surprise, but Minny jumped completely out of her chair, declaring, "Be calm, everyone! My husband was a volunteer fireman!"

Before she could be reassured that strawberries flambé was supposed to be aflame, Minny dragged her considerable sleeve across the blazing dessert to retrieve a finger bowl. Before she could grab it, her sleeve began to smolder.

"Mother—" Angela launched herself upward "—you're on fire!"

"Oh! Heaven preserve me!" Minny yelped. In her panic, she yanked at the front of her jumpsuit, ripping it apart in her frenzy to be free of the smoking fabric. Buttons flew like shrapnel. One plopped into the dessert. One hit Angela in the shoulder as she ran to her mother. One went pinging into a crystal goblet after ricocheting off a fork.

Tarrant hurriedly dunked his linen napkin in his fingerbowl and, rounding the table, caught Minny about the waist and corralled her long enough to smother the smoking muslin with the napkin. Angela arrived then, pushing back the sleeve to see if her mother was burned.

Immediately, Tarrant, Minny and Angela were surrounded by the others. Not seeing any physical damage to her mother's skin, Angela gathered the gaping bodice together, though Minny wore a modest camisole beneath it, and cried, "Are you all right?"

Minny blinked first at her daughter and then up at her savior, moaning weakly. "Son. You saved my life."

Tarrant was grim, almost pale under his tan. Obviously, the near debacle had shaken him. "Hardly that," he corrected. "Are you in pain anywhere?"

Minny fluttered her lashes. "Oh, I do believe I'm going to swoon— My heart . . ."

"Good gracious," Delila declared. "Get her into bed, Tarrant. I'll call a doctor."

Tarrant swept the limp woman into his arms and carried her away.

SOMETIME LATER, after the doctor had gone, Angela was alone in a grandly appointed bedroom with her invalid mother. Minny was languishing beneath a champagne-colored satin comforter, munching contentedly on chocolate-covered strawberries.

"Mother," Angela protested worriedly, "are you sure you should be eating? What did the doctor say?"

Minny licked chocolate from her fingers before she replied, "He said I had a bad scare, but that I'm fine." Giving Angela a sly wink, she added, "Besides, you know I have a good, strong heart. Always have."

Angela sat back on the bed, looking confused. "I thought you . . ."

Minny rummaged about in the confection box, searching for just the right piece of candy before she lifted her gaze back to her daughter's stricken face. "Sweetie. You and I both know that you're going to marry Tarrant Seaton on May twenty-third. I just decided I'd help Cupid along a little by giving you two some extra time together. That's all."

Angela started to speak, but she was so dumbfounded she couldn't find her voice. In an incredulous whisper, she finally managed, "Mother! That's . . . that's deceitful!"

With an elfish smile, Minny popped a piece of candy into her mouth.

CHAPTER SIX

HORRIFIED, ANGELA BOLTED from the bed. "We can't stay here, Mother! I won't take the Seatons' hospitality under false pretenses!"

Minny cautioned her daughter to be quiet, waving her to sit back down. "Now, now, sweetie. You know I can't leave tonight. Delila sent my jumpsuit to her seamstress. It won't be back until tomorrow morning."

"But..." Angela faltered. Would it be any better to have to borrow clothes and make a hasty exit at this hour—almost eleven o'clock? They'd only have to further disturb Delila, who had already retired to her room.

Heaving a restrained sigh, Angela shook her head. "All right, Mother. We'll stay. But your subterfuge isn't going to work, because I saw Tarrant Seaton leave with Eden once they got the news that you were going to be fine." She paced toward the door, then returned to the bed. "I hope you're satisfied."

Minny's smile had vanished. "Daughter, you can't think I set fire to myself *on purpose*. That was an accident. But when Tarrant was holding me and looking so upset, the idea just popped into my head."

Angela sighed again. "Well, it's done now." Then she said dejectedly, "If you think you'll be okay, I'm going to my room."

Minny fluffed the lace at the neckline of the silk gown Delila had lent her. She looked like some dowager queen, propped up on snow-white pillows with hand-crocheted edging, as she lounged in that massive bed with its ceiling-high, heirloom headboard.

Minny cast her animated gaze about her and purred with satisfaction. "You know? I could get used to this bedroom."

"Don't get too attached to it," Angela advised. "It wouldn't fit into our apartment. As a matter of fact, I think our apartment would fit in here."

Minny giggled. "I do believe it would."

Her emotions still in turmoil, Angela bent down and kissed her mother's cheek, murmuring, "Go right to sleep. And please, don't to anything like this again. If you do, I'll have a hard time convincing myself that Mr. Seaton is wrong in his accusations about us!"

Minny suddenly appeared genuinely hurt. "Now, Angela, you must remember that the fates are in complete control here. Your marriage to that wonderful, wonderful boy is destined. So never think negative thoughts about your wedding! I'm as certain it will happen as I am that Nancy Reagan will write a book about her life."

"She already has, Mother."

"There, you see?" Minny spread her arms in an it's-out-of-my-hands gesture. "The fates have spoken!"

Angela grimaced and closed her eyes, hoping that counting to ten would help. After a minute, she said, "Good night, Mother. Sleep well."

"I simply couldn't help sleeping well in this bed," Minny cooed as she settled back on the pillows.

Angela flipped off the light and moved across the hall to her room. The pale blue-and-eggshell bedroom was also elegant, with a four-poster bed surrounded by airy lace curtains. Angela could hardly believe the opulence in which some people lived. For a long moment she merely turned in a slow circle, admiring everything from the quaint rolltop desk beside the bed to the carved and gilt mirror over the dressing table.

It was a fairyland, and she felt like Cinderella. Unfortunately, the handsome prince was not only engaged to someone else, but he was a coldhearted cad. Besides, she reminded herself, she didn't even like him!

Pushing all thoughts of Tarrant Seaton out of her mind, Angela decided to change into the delicate negligee that had been draped across the bedspread. Before she could unbutton her dress, she realized she was hungry. That didn't surprise her. She hadn't eaten much at dinner, and, since she'd skipped lunch, her stomach had every right to complain.

She figured she probably wouldn't do the Seaton fortune much damage by making herself a snack, so she headed down to the kitchen. Rummaging in the industrial-size refrigerator, Angela came up with the ingredients for a hefty turkey sandwich.

She wrapped a paper towel around her sandwich and began to munch as she walked out the kitchen door. She ambled down the steps to the moonlit grounds, giving in to her restlessness.

Glancing about, she got her bearings. She'd emerged from the house at the edge of a small pine wood. Far off to one side, she could see the patio fountain sparkle with reflected moonlight. The temperature was noticeably cooler near the wood, so she chose to stroll through the trees. Even here, the lawn was clipped to golf-course perfection, making walking among the pines a thoroughly enjoyable experience.

The soft scent of roses and wild honeysuckle permeated the sharp tang of the pines. She wandered aimlessly, nibbling occasionally on her snack and smiling up at the moon as it glewed placidly down through the still branches.

As she turned back toward the mansion, feeling refreshed and at long last composed, she was startled to see a bright ball of light jumping in the distance. It appeared to be getting closer. She stopped, her heart thumping. What was it? She'd heard of ball lightning, but she'd never seen it. Could this be that odd natural phenomenon?

Suddenly, she heard a harsh, masculine shout. "Halt! Don't move! My dog is trained to attack anybody who runs."

"Oh, my lord!" she mouthed soundlessly, going so still she didn't even dare breathe. Now she could see that the bouncing light was a flashlight carried by a man in some kind of uniform. The moon gave off enough light for her to discern the glint of knee-high boots and the bill of a hat—and the teeth of a huge, growling Doberman.

"All right, lady," the uniformed man snarled as he reached her. "Why don't we just go back to where we came from? This is no place for you to be prowling." As he spoke, he tucked his flashlight into a slot on his belt, then none too gently took her by the arm and began pulling her toward the mansion.

"What... what do you think you're doing?" Angela sputtered. "I... I was just out for a walk!"

"Sure, sure," he snickered. "You dames are all alike. I never seen such a thing in my life. Once, twice a week, yet!"

Angela was scared. She didn't like the look of the dog straining at his leash beside her captor. Though obviously well-trained, the animal was eyeing her—or maybe her turkey sandwich—greedily. A thought rushed through her mind. What if she tossed the sandwich into the darkness?

It might deflect the dog's attention long enough for her to jerk free and make an escape.

Then she envisioned the probable consequences of such a rash escape attempt. She saw herself pitched facedown in the grass, a snarling beast's fangs attached to her backside. Squeezing her eyes shut to squelch the gruesome image, Angela discarded all thoughts of flight. Feeling thwarted, she protested her captivity with a yank of the man's hold. "Take your hands off me!" she demanded. "I don't know who you think you are, but I don't appreciate being called a dame!"

The man laughed. "Yeah. Get huffy. They all do." He continued to drag her along as he talked. "I suppose you're going to tell me you're here at Mr. Seaton's invitation."

She fixed him with a grim stare, retorting, "Of course I'm here at his invitation!"

He chortled. "Honey, I think I'd drop over dead if one of you ever came up with a new one. Now, Mr. Seaton's orders is not to press charges, so where's your car? I'll just escort you to it and you can be on your way."

Angela planted her feet, forgetting about the woman-eating hound. "I won't go. My mother's inside." To illustrate, she waved her sandwich toward the mansion, insisting, "My mother and I are Mr. Seaton's guests." Without her realizing, her voice was getting shrill and loud. She'd never been so ill-treated before. "How dare you suggest that I've done anything against the law!"

"Trespassing's not exactly something you put on your résumé, lady."

"I'm not trespassing!" she persisted, shouting now. "Go inside and ask Delila Seaton! I'm a houseguest!"

"Right. And I'm Prince Charles," he sneered.

"What's going on out there, Bentley?" a baritone voice called from the patio. Angela knew right away that it was Tarrant, and though she didn't care to be in his debt, she yelled, "This lout is hauling me out to the street, Mr. Seaton!"

There was silence for a minute, when Angela could not only hear the distant cry of an owl, but her own thumping heart.

Finally Tarrant called, "Bring the culprit here, Bentley."

"Well, sugar, you might just get lucky." The man turned to inspect Angela. His eyes were hidden in shadow by the bill of his hat, but his teeth flashed lewdly. "'Course, I can see why. You're a real looker."

She sniffed, offended, and pulled out of his grip. "Do you mind? I can walk by myself."

He kept very near, saying, "You run, sugar, and I'll let Lunatic chase you down. He *loves* to play chase."

Angela swallowed, but tried not to let the horrid man see her trepidation. When she and Bentley reached the stairs leading up to the broad patio, Tarrant was standing on the top step, hands planted casually on his hips. He'd removed his sports coat and loosened his tie, but he was still dressed as he had been at dinner. Apparently he hadn't lingered with Eden.

His expression was highly amused, and even in the dimness, she could see the twinkle of laughter in his eyes. "Why, hello there, Miss Meadows. Fancy meeting you here. What were you doing—looking for my balcony?"

She halted, but was rammed from the rear by the obnoxious Bentley. The impact almost knocked her to her knees.

"I found another one of those women, boss," Bentley explained as he steadied her rather roughly.

Angela jerked her arm from his hold, not sure which emotion was more inflamed—her fury or her embarrassment.

Tarrant was coming down the steps toward them. When he reached Bentley, he petted the dog's big head and addressed the guard. "You've done good work, Bentley, but I think you and Lunatic can leave this one to me."

Angela shot a deadly glance at her host. He pursed his lips in an obvious attempt to mask his humor, but his eyes glistened with remorseless mirth at her expense.

She blustered, "This man should be severely chastised! He...he manhandled me!"

"Will that be all, boss?" Bentley asked, apparently far from panicked by her charge.

"Yes." Tarrant nodded. "Keep up the vigilant work."

The man about-faced and, along with the faithful Lunatic, strode off. Angela watched him go, her mouth open. When the guard and his dog were out of earshot, she spun around and protested, "Does that brute work for you?"

Tarrant crossed his arms and gave her a cool look. "That brute works for me, yes."

"Well...well, how can you keep a beast like that on? I'll have you know he almost broke my arm!"

Tarrant's expression became skeptical, but he asked, "Which arm?"

She started to show him, then changed her mind. "You don't care! Why should I show you?"

He flashed her a wry grin. "Be obstinate if you want. But I'd suggest you don't go wandering around the grounds after dark anymore. We don't have a security system for nothing."

"If you ask me, you don't have a security system, you have a pack of dirty-minded baby-sitters. Where do you find your guards? The National Institute of Jerks? And

Lunatic? A perfect name, I might add! That hound from hell wanted to kill me!''

"That dog's a pussycat."

"Well, somebody'd better tell him! He didn't act like he wanted to leap into my lap and purr!"

With a casual nod of his head, he indicated the patio. "Why don't we go sit down? It's been a long day."

She balked, her pride still bruised from her ordeal. "No, thank you, Mr. Seaton. I'm going to bed."

"Why don't you call me Tarrant, Angela? After all we've been through together, I think we're past the formal stage."

His radical change of subject caught her off guard. "I, uh..." She felt suddenly shy, awkward. Why? What was the problem with calling this man by his first name? Somehow it bothered her to hear him say hers. Not caring to face the possible reasons for this, she mumbled, "Whatever..."

His low chuckle seemed loud in the night's quiet. "You're a strange case. I mean, with your mother's ploy to stay here overnight, I expected to see you, but I didn't expect to see you quite this way."

Angela blanched. So he knew it was a ploy! How was she to defend herself? She stared down at her toes, knowing how guilty she looked.

"Well?" he prompted, making her jump.

She squirmed. There was no way she could answer him. She certainly had no intention of blaming her mother. Even if she did, he'd just chastise her for trying to foist the blame onto someone else. He'd done it before, and this time the circumstances were much more damaging.

Gathering her courage, she met his critical gaze, responding defiantly, "My mother didn't set herself on fire on purpose."

He lifted one eyebrow, but didn't respond. She wanted to stalk off, not caring to prolong her time under his cynical scrutiny, but a question nagged at her. Finally her curiosity won out and she asked, "What did that security thug mean when he said he found 'another one of those women'?"

A smile, fleeting and humorless, skipped across his mouth. "Women like you, bent on matrimony." His voice was cold. "Only the others didn't have the help of two interfering coconspirators—namely your mother and, unintentionally, mine."

"You're not trying to tell me women sneak in here to... to get you to..." She was too stunned to finish. The picture this idea presented made her blush, and she was glad for the cover of darkness. "I don't believe that," she insisted stiffly, not sure if she was upset because he thought so little of her character, or because he had so much late-night feminine company!

His narrowed eyes gauged her carefully for a long minute. His expression, rugged and rakish in the moonlight, was unreadable. Then he shoved his hands into his pockets. "You're good at playing the wide-eyed innocent, Angela. I'll give you that," he said with disturbing candor.

She started to object, but before she could say anything, he inquired, "Tell me, has Minny had any revelations about our honeymoon?"

Taking a deep breath, Angela declared, "Let me put it this way, *Tarrant*—" the emphasis on his given name made it sound like blasphemy "—if I'm ever forced into such a revolting event, I hope you and I are on separate continents at the time!" Eyeing him grudgingly, she asked, "Are you hungry?"

He looked puzzled. "A little. Why?"

"Because I've just lost my appetite, and I have a sandwich." Thrusting it at him, she snapped, "Turkey!"

Brushing past him, she hurried toward the mansion's patio entrance. After she'd gone a few steps, she heard him call, "Don't think you can sway me with sweet talk, Angela." His voice was edged with ill-concealed laughter. She cursed him for his ceaseless penchant for mocking her.

MORNING SEEMED to take forever to come. Angela had tossed and turned and stared out the window until dawn. For some demented reason her mind insisted on recalling Tarrant's face—that deep-cleft chin, those sinful lashes and that hedonistic smile....

She was restless and wanted to get up and walk off her frustrations, but she didn't care to chance running into Bentley again—or Lunatic. Finally, she busied herself showering, cleaning the bathroom, dressing, stripping the bed and then pacing, hoping the maid would come soon to tell her where clean sheets were kept so she could make the bed.

After what felt like an eternity, there was a soft knock at the door. A frilly-frocked maid entered the room and was startled to see the bed ready for clean sheets. Though she didn't want Angela to make the bed, she finally compromised and allowed her to help. As they worked, the maid introduced herself as Peg, and proceeded to chatter away.

"That Miss Eden is a lovely lady," Peg said, smoothing the sheet.

"Yes, she is," Angela agreed.

"Took her divorce hard, I understand," the maid offered, peering over at Angela.

"Oh?"

Peg nodded and spoke confidentially. "I understand there was another woman."

Angela didn't care to gossip about Eden, so she changed the subject. "You need to pull the sheet your way a little. It's dragging the floor over here."

The maid heaved a histrionic sigh at Angela's perfectionism and began tugging at the fabric. "Anyway, Miss Eden is in Mr. Tarrant's social circle, and she's rich as a movie star, so she's not after his fortune." As she arranged the bedspread, Peg paused to give Angela a narrow look. "Not like *some* women."

Angela would have had to be unconscious to miss the accusation in Peg's remark. Still not accustomed to being thought of as a money-grubbing bimbo, she lowered her gaze, pretending to adjust the bedspread on her side. She hated being in this crazy situation. She wasn't that kind of woman at all! But she had too much pride to start an argument with the maid. Instead, she stood, brushed an invisible speck from her dress and smiled at the stiff-faced woman. "Well, that's done. I think I'll go down to breakfast."

The maid offered a false smile.

Unhappily, Angela knew that the maid would love to see her head served up on a platter, so she said honestly, "You're very loyal to Mr. Seaton. That's commendable for an employee."

"Of course I am. He's a fine man," the maid countered. "And he's too nice for his own good, I'd say."

Angela frowned. Too nice? Tarrant Seaton? The terms seemed mutually exclusive. Shaking her head, she murmured, "You couldn't prove it by me," and walked away. Within the hour she'd be able to leave. She only hoped Tarrant would have the good grace to have his breakfast in his room.

Her hopes were dashed the moment she reached the plant-filled sun room off the kitchen. There he was, resplendent in, of all things, gray sweats. He looked so tousled and cuddly that the sight took her breath away. How in the world could a man in sweatpants, sweatshirt and a pair of running shoes do such brazen things to her heart? Especially a scoundrel with a wicked grin and a condescending wit.

Delila was there, too, clad in a majestic high-necked robe. "Good morning, my dear," she said, beckoning Angela to a seat opposite Minny. Angela noted with relief that her mother was wearing her repaired jumpsuit. She didn't know if it was bad planning or simply bad luck, but she found herself sitting all too near Tarrant, who was taking up two spaces by propping a foot on the end chair.

"Good morning, Angela," he said, his expression polite, his undertone teasing. "Sleep well?"

"Like a rock," she lied with an equally polite smile. "I presume you've been pumping iron? Or maybe practising for the Boston marathon?"

"Neither. Just relaxing." He stretched languidly, looking suddenly far more lethal than cuddly. "Even chocolate maggots relax."

"You left out 'humorous,'" she reminded him with false sweetness.

"You flatter me, but thanks," he replied with a devilish flash of teeth, turning her planned slur into a compliment. "You're just in time, Angela. Minny was about to relate a dream she had last night."

Angela sent a distressed gaze toward her mother, who was drizzling honey onto a croissant.

"You had a dream, Mother?" Angela asked weakly.

"Oh, yes. Quite a confusing dream."

"Confusing?" Tarrant put in, a puzzled note in his voice. "For you, Mrs. Meadows? I find that hard to conceive."

Angela shot him a deadly look. He was ridiculing her mother! Unfortunately, she couldn't accuse him of it outright, for his face exhibited nothing but quiet interest.

Though Angela was fighting back her indignation, Minny had apparently missed the disguised censure. She giggled. "Aren't you sweet, son, but listen to it and I think you'll agree."

With an indulgent expression, Delila assured Minny, "I'm intrigued. What did you dream?"

Minny took a bite of her croissant, using the moment to heighten suspense. Angela cast a disheartened glance at her plate, where an artfully arranged half cantaloupe filled with strawberries sat beside a bran muffin and a croissant. It certainly looked like a breakfast one might have in a mansion. Bustling servants came and went, bringing in covered dishes and replenishing coffee. It was clear that the plate of fruit and pastries was only the beginning.

"Quite confusing," Minny repeated, blotting her lips with her napkin. "I dreamed of a sailor riding a lion into the sea, and he was singing a song. The only words of the song I can recall were, 'A dilly, a dilly adieu—'"

Delila gasped. She tipped the cup she was holding, sloshing coffee across her plate. As all eyes turned to her, she smiled feebly and murmured, "Forgive an old woman's clumsiness." When a maid hurried to clear her ruined breakfast and replace it with a fresh one, Delila prompted, "Please, Minny, go on."

"Well..." Minny sipped her coffee absently. "I've thought a lot about this and I believe I've come up with its meaning."

Angela chewed on a strawberry, watching her mother, and hoping this would soon be over with no damage done. She prayed inwardly that nothing—absolutely not one syllable—would be uttered about a marriage between Tarrant and her. After his accusation last night, she'd just die!

"You see, the lion in my dreams represents Leo, or actually the months of July and August, and the sailor most certainly symbolizes the ocean or water, which I've deduced represents rain. And the song, 'Dilly, dilly adieu,' tells me in no uncertain terms that the summer will be so rainy that cucumbers will not do well and the dill-pickle industry will suffer." She grinned broadly.

Tarrant coughed behind his napkin, and Delila sat back, the rigidity around her mouth softening. Angela remained motionless and worried.

"That is enlightening," Tarrant observed. "Perhaps I'd better sell my dill-pickle stock." He lifted a brow speculatively, adding, "I hope no one accuses me of insider trading."

That did it! Angela had endured enough of Tarrant's gibes and innuendoes, and—though she felt disloyal admitting it even to herself—her mother's antics had stretched her nerves to the breaking point. She simply couldn't take any more of this! Desperate, she abruptly stood, faced Delila and stated with all the sincerity she could muster, "It was wonderful of you to allow Mother to rest here last night. And the jumpsuit looks perfect." While she fabricated an excuse, Angela hurried around the table, urging her mother up from her chair. "And breakfast was delicious. But I simply have to get to the store. Expecting some shipments...you understand."

"I do understand, my dear," Delila returned, too lady-like to become ruffled by Angela's impetuous rush to leave. "Tarrant, love, see our guests to the door."

He was already on his feet. "My pleasure, Mother," he murmured, his eyes narrowed with lazy humor. Folding Minny's arm over his, he escorted her to the mansion's front entrance, forcing Angela to trail behind them.

"I'll check into that pickle problem, Minny," Tarrant promised, no doubt to fuel Angela's anger.

"Do that, son. I'd hate to see your fortune go down the drain due to a bad cucumber harvest." At the door, she scurried outside toward their car.

When Tarrant stepped aside to allow Angela to follow her mother, his gaze caught hers. "Adieu, Angela," he taunted, his lips twisting in a flawless, tormenting grin.

His physical perfection forced Angela to take a self-protective step backward. He was so bold, so magnetic and so infuriating! "You think you're cute, I suppose?" she hissed.

He laughed; the rich sound of it was as intense and warm as the prairie sun. "Since you ask, Angela, I've been told I'm damned cute."

At the end of her emotional tether and too miserable to guard her words, she retorted, "Oh? Well, I've been told that some women will say *anything* to get a man's money!"

Like a lantern dashed to earth in the wind, the teasing fire in his eyes exploded and died.

CHAPTER SEVEN

DELILA LOOKED UP as Tarrant reentered the sun room. She seemed somewhat bemused. "That was certainly a hasty exit. Did they get off safely?"

Taking his place at the table, Tarrant nodded, frowning. "Yes, but if you ask me, they've been 'off' for quite some time."

Delila laughed at his joke. "I know, I really enjoy Minny. She's so completely devoid of guile. It's refreshing."

Tarrant eyed his mother skeptically. "So are you, darling."

With a surprised lift of her brows she asked, "So am I what? Devoid of guile or refreshing?"

His lips twitched, but without humor. "Both perhaps, because in my opinion, Minny and Angela are crafty females."

Delila's face clouded with distress as he went on, "That young one is so underhanded she appears completely honest." The irony of his own remark drew a reluctant grunt of amusement from him.

"You're wrong, Tarrant. She's sweet. Truly sweet. I don't think she's a thing like those other women who've tried to catch you with trickery."

Tarrant took a bite of his melon, then shifted his dark gaze back to meet his mother's. "Oh? And from what crystal ball did you come by that conclusion?"

Delila's expression grew contemplative. "No crystal ball, my love. Just the wisdom of many years." Laying aside her fork, she sat back and sighed. "Tarrant, you are my son and I love you above all else. And I can see that it has been your unfortunate fate to have a, well, rather masterful physical presence—"

"Mother, I doubt—"

With a wave of her hand she halted his attempted denial. "Hush, Tarrant, and let me speak. You can't think me so naive that I haven't noticed the effect you have on women." She paused. "I haven't always been an old woman, dear. I, too, have been affected by the magnetism of the opposite sex. I know very well that the drive to mate is strong."

"Mother, if you're about to tell me the facts of life—" Tarrant started to protest.

"I dare say you already know," she interjected with a raised eyebrow. "Don't distract me. As I was trying to explain, there are men that some women will do anything to obtain." She stopped, looked away and then met his eyes again. "I sincerely doubt Angela is one of those women. But whatever the case, I hope you can develop compassion for people—men or women—who possess less strength of character than you. You might be surprised..." She allowed the sentence to drift away before clearing her throat.

He watched her for a long, silent moment before he asked, "I might be surprised about what, Mother?"

Appearing uncharacteristically restless, she stood and brushed at an imaginary wrinkle in her satin robe. "Nothing. Never mind, dear. Just think about what I've said." With that, she hurried out and left Tarrant sitting alone in the sun room.

He scowled at the gardens extending beyond the window. After a protracted silence, he shoved his plate away, muttering to no one in particular, "What the hell *did* she say?"

ANGELA PULLED to a grinding halt in the Delila's Delights employee parking lot. The *Seatonville Herald*'s morning headline forced its way into her brain for the hundredth time: "Prince of Delights to Marry."

She saw again the two large photos—one, a familiar publicity shot of Tarrant, smiling that devilish grin, the second, of sweet pale Eden Leslie. At last the announcement of their engagement was public knowledge.

Feeling a strange twinge not unlike regret, she reminded herself this was for the best. But she wondered if her mother would ever let it go. Minny had ranted all through breakfast as though Tarrant had left Angela standing at the church!

With a hearty shove, she opened her car door and stepped out onto the blacktop. Minny's dream about their marriage had been crazy. Another good example of the idiocy of Minny's predictions had been that screwy tale about the sailor riding a lion into the ocean. The truth was that both she and Minny had made fools of themselves— more than once—in front of Tarrant Seaton. She blushed as all the painful memories flooded back.

"Well, well, if it isn't *Mrs.* Tarrant Seaton!" a voice scoffed behind Angela. She'd expected some ribbing at the factory today, but she'd assumed she'd at least get inside the building before it started.

As she turned she accidently bumped into Marty, knocking her notebook and lunch to the ground, along with Marty's smock and several things she'd been carrying.

"Look what you've done, Miss Clumsy," Marty rebuked. "Doesn't seem like you can do anything right, does it?"

Not wanting a confrontation, Angela bent to retrieve the fallen belongings as the redhead prompted with a sneer, "So, how does it feel to get dumped?"

Fumbling to balance two lunch sacks, a smock, a notebook, two purses and Marty's half-eaten Danish, Angela stood and whispered, "Please, let's not do this. Leave it be."

Marty laughed. "You thought you were so high and mighty. Thought you were going to catch the really big fish."

Angela didn't want to get involved in a shouting match. Glancing around, she could see that Marty's shrill accusations were attracting a crowd.

"Give me my things," the redhead spat, grabbing at Angela's jumbled collection. With a defiant jerk of her head, she declared, "You know, Tarrant's been engaged before."

Marty's suddenly strained tone stopped Angela from what she'd been about to say. It was clear that Marty had fixated on the idea that the Prince of Delights would someday, somehow, notice her and sweep her away on his white charger. Angela was stunned to realize that Marty had actually deluded herself into believing that romantic notion. Feeling helpless, she tried, "I know the tabloids make a point of reporting his wild flings, Marty, but this time, with Eden—"

"Oh, shut up! Just because he dumped you, you don't have to rain on my parade!" Snatching the sack lunch Angela was holding, Marty dropped it to the pavement and stomped gleefully on it, crowing, "There! What superior, brilliant remark do you have to make now, Miss Smarty-Pants?''

Angela stared openmouthed at the mushy mess before she met Marty's smug expression. Clearing her throat, she said, ''I don't know what to say, Marty, except, maybe... *bon appétit?*''

''What is that supposed to mean?'' Marty snapped.

Halfheartedly, Angela held up a bag that had been hidden behind her notebook, murmuring, ''Unfortunately, it means... that was your lunch.''

The redhead's face hardened with fury, but the titter of laughter around her seemed to prevent her from pursuing her argument. With a low growl, she slunk away.

Angela clutched her notebook and lunch to her chest and headed into the building. Glimpsing herself in the chrome of the elevator door, she noticed that her cheeks had gone flame red with indignation and she felt a surge of irritation. Because of Tarrant Seaton, she'd been caused more than her share of grief for one day.

ANGELA HAD BEEN AT WORK for more than eight hours without a break. She'd struggled through dank unused storage areas, measuring, moving crates full of outdated files, digging into stale recesses, sketching, sneezing and becoming coated with dust.

At long last, unable to straighten up without groaning, she decided it was time to finish for the day. She stepped out of the last of the seven storage areas that were to be remodeled and took the elevator to the main level, surprised to notice it was dark outside.

With a tired sigh, she looked down at herself. She'd started out that morning looking neat in a pair of navy slacks and a matching cotton shirt. Now, however, the slacks were streaked with dust, cobwebs dangled from her shirt, and she felt grimy.

Her car was at the other side of the factory. She began the trek down the long hall trying not to think about how much her feet hurt. Her shoes echoed hollowly, giving her an eerie feeling. It was odd to be so utterly alone in such a vast building.

As she trudged along, Angela became aware that other footsteps were approaching. She looked behind her. The hall wasn't brightly lit, and she saw nothing.

Nor was there anyone ahead. She stopped, listening. The other footfalls continued—clipped, heavier than hers, and growing louder.

It was no more than a few seconds before a shadowy figure turned a corner, almost colliding with her. The apparition came to an abrupt halt, and she bit down hard on her lip when she realized who it was.

The Prince of Delights towered there, dressed with understated elegance in a charcoal-gray suit, the trim pleated trousers accentuating his considerable height. His matching suede shoes were lush and classic. His shirt was white washed silk, his patterned tie silk crepe. From his shoulders billowed a long black raincoat, and tucked under one arm, he carried a black umbrella. All in all, the ensemble shouted tasteful extravagance.

When he recognized her, his expression suddenly darkened, then just as suddenly, his lips lifted in a wry grin. "Angela, I don't believe I've ever seen you look more...charming."

His sarcasm stung. And she was too tired to put up with anymore. "You're a very clever man, Tarrant. You should teach a class—sarcasm 101."

His laughter rankled. "There must be something to reverse psychology. I could swear from the look on your face that you despise me, and blast it, that's intriguing."

Before she could fathom his intentions, he had taken her briefcase and set it on the floor beside his umbrella. Then, with determined authority, he gathered her into his arms and brought his mouth down on hers.

Bewildered, she blinked in shock as his lips slid seductively across hers. *He was kissing her—actually kissing her. An engaged man!* His kiss was demanding, reproachful, taunting, and she pressed against his chest, moaning out her distress. How could he treat her so shabbily?

"Please, no..." she choked out a broken whisper, but he was having none of it. His arms held her securely to him, and he seemed not to hear her tormented cry. Though caught in the grip of guilt and remorse, Angela noticed a subtle change in his manner, as if something in their shared kiss had taken him by surprise.

Lifting his lips for the briefest second, he chided, "You play the game very well, Angela." His tone, husky and edged with passion, sent a frightened shiver along her spine. He was so attractive, so eloquent in his lovemaking, that resisting him was a feat of monumental difficulty. She doubted that many women had succeeded in denying him anything he wanted.

When his mouth took possession of hers again, her lashes fluttered closed. Tears of regret trailed down her face, and she damned herself inwardly for her weakness. Still trying to resist, she found herself unable to struggle any longer. He nipped gently at her lower lip, and she groaned with unwanted pleasure. Without permission, her hands slid beneath his jacket, her fingers skimmed along the sleekness of his shirt, making her acutely aware of a virile body beneath the rich fabric.

She had never expected to know Tarrant's kiss, and she had never imagined that the experience would affect her in such a crazy way. She felt dizzy, and her body tingled with strange sensations that were foreign yet exciting.

Instinctively, she moved her mouth lower to kiss his jaw. A thrill of delight ran through her as he explored the tender skin along the edge of her ear.

Their impetuous kiss suddenly seemed so natural, so glorious, so wildly right! Unthinking, uncaring, Angela smiled inwardly as her lips moved again to meet Tarrant's, which were now softly caressing, showing a tenderness she'd never suspected.

Then, abruptly, he let her go, growling a curse. All she could do was stagger backward, wide-eyed and feeling bereft, disoriented.

In a harsh voice he demanded, "Everyone knew I'd be working late, Miss Meadows. By showing up here and melting into my arms with just the right amount of ladylike unwillingness, am I to understand that there can be side benefits for me while you're working for my mother?"

Still muddled and breathless, Angela was confused by his biting remark. "What do you..." Before she could get the question out, she realized he was suggesting that *she* wanted a sleazy affair with him! Thunderstruck that he would make such a cruel remark at her expense, she said tightly, "The next time you want to be humorous, Mr. Seaton, put on a red nose and big floppy shoes. You might get more laughs!"

The calculating glint in his eyes died as she launched herself past him and beat a hasty retreat. All the way to the exit, his dark, angry face remained etched in her mind's eye. But why did she have the irrational feeling that he was more provoked with himself than with her?

Angela's emotions were in chaos as she scurried out into a gloomy drizzle, trying valiantly not to burst into tears. So what if Tarrant Seaton was engaged! So what if he felt nothing but contempt for her! So what if his kiss had given her a glimpse of an intoxicating realm she'd never imagined possible—a realm he would never invite her to fully and lovingly explore! *So what!*

So, why was she crying—stupid, silly idiot that she was?

A WEEK LATER, Angela returned to the Seaton mansion to continue her work. She couldn't put it off any longer. Delila had called at the last minute, inviting Minny to spend the afternoon and then join her for a trip into Wichita to see a play.

With Minny and Delila off chatting in the sun room, Angela went about her work, relieved to know that Tarrant was "seeing to some property" and wouldn't be back until evening.

"Well, sweetie," Minny called from the top of the basement stairs, "Delila and I are leaving for Wichita."

Angela stepped out of the storage space where she was examining a carpenter's progress and waved. "Now, don't you two get into any trouble."

Minny chortled. "Delila's going to drop me off at the apartment after the play. But don't wait up. We might pick up a couple of cool duds."

This time it was Angela's turn to laugh. "I think you mean dudes, Mother." She paused, then added, "On second thought, just have a good time."

"Right off, dudette!"

Angela shook her head and went on with her inspection. "Right off, Mother," she muttered, thinking Minny was probably not too far wrong—dudette, indeed! She'd felt very much like a dudette since Tarrant had so rudely kissed her.

She hadn't really thought about it until then, but she had to face the fact that her social life was nothing short of nonexistent. She'd been too busy to notice when an interested male had smiled at her. And having been forced, at Tarrant's expert hands, to experience the possibilities that existed between a man and a woman, she'd begun to feel oddly discontented. Darn that Tarrant Seaton! Why couldn't he have just growled at her as usual? Why did he have to . . .

She shook her head. Dwelling on something she couldn't do anything about was fruitless. She squared her shoulders staunchly and turned back to her work, driving herself hard. It was the best way she knew to force uninvited thoughts of the Prince of Delights from her brain.

Some time later, Angela checked her watch. It was nearly seven o'clock. The plasterers and carpenters were packing up. There was little she could do once they were gone, so she decided to call it a day, too.

She phoned Richard at the store, where he was just closing up, and was relieved that all had gone well. No horrible problems, except for the mistaken delivery of twelve hundred pink plastic drawer knobs. Richard had handled it, though, refusing to pay the COD charge and insisting the cheap knobs be returned.

"Good work, Richard," she complimented him, rubbing her neck and trying not to sound weary. "I'll see you at ten tomorrow. There's nothing more I can do out here until the rest of the custom modules are shipped from Kansas City. Thanks for holding down the fort."

The gravel road between the Seaton mansion and Seatonville was so familiar to Angela by now that she hardly paid attention to it, her thoughts trailing along other avenues—her store, her vast assignment from Delila's Delights, Tarrant...

Before she was even aware that there was anything wrong, Angela's foot was slamming down on her brake pedal as a pickup truck carrying wire crates full of live chickens materialized at a crossroad.

She had plenty of time to stop, but for some reason, her brake pedal wasn't responding to her frantic stomping.

"Oh, no!" she cried as her car rolled into the path of the pickup and collided with its left front fender, making a sickening metallic crunch.

Her car came to a belated halt thanks to the impact, and when it did, she heard an ominous hissing as her front end began to settle slowly earthward.

The farmer, red-faced and incensed, leapt from the cab of his truck, ranting and gesticulating as he inspected his crumpled fender.

"And look at my chickens!" he wailed.

Angela, who'd been paralyzed by shock, lifted frightened eyes in the direction he was pointing. She was distressed to see that a number of the crates had toppled out of the truck into the muddy gully beside the road. Rust-colored chickens had escaped and were squawking and skittering in all directions. If it hadn't been such an awful mess, it might have been funny.

"Hey, you there," the farmer shouted, waving a thick finger at her. "What're you gonna do—sit there? I just bought these hens. You scared 'em silly. Help me catch 'em before they run off."

She dragged a shaky hand through her hair, wincing at a bump on her forehead. Surprised, she realized she'd hit the steering wheel during the accident, and now her head was beginning to ache. With great effort, she managed to get her door opened and began to chase down frightened chickens through fields, ankle-deep in mud.

"You get that big 'un over there," the farmer yelled. "She's a prize layin' hen."

Angela nodded and slogged through the mud, her ruined pumps bogging her down. Just as she was about to coax the big bird into her arms, Angela stepped into a hole and went down face first. The hen squawked and darted adroitly away.

Angela came up coughing and sputtering, pulling a feather from her mouth. "Ugh!" she cried. Using the back of her wrist, she cleared her eyes of mud.

"Dang it, lady. Ya missed her."

Angela grimaced, tasting mud. "I know. I'll get her," she said through grime-spattered lips.

Thirty minutes later, the farmer was tenderly taking the last rescued chicken from Angela's mud-caked arms.

"It's a dang good thing they ain't hurt, young woman," he muttered. "These girls are prize Rhode Island Reds. I got kids to feed and a farm to run. Wouldn't do to have these girls out of commission."

Angela, her head pounding, nodded again, repeating for the twentieth time, "I'm sorry, Mr., er..."

"Kilgore," he said. "And just what are you going to do 'bout my truck?"

Pressing her hands to her throbbing temples, she assured him, "Of course, I'll pay for any damage." She knew the accident had been her fault, and she didn't blame Mr. Kilgore for being angry, but his bellowing wasn't doing her head any good.

The farmer looked away from Angela, squinting down the road. She heard it then and turned, too. The sound of hoofbeats was coming their way. A huge black stallion with its darkly clad rider galloped toward them, like a phantom from Kansas's wild past. The rider, Stetson pulled low on his brow, rode smoothly and expertly, and something about the spread of the cowboy's wide shoulders galvanized a thought in Angela's mind. No, it was impossible. She dismissed the notion as giddiness caused by being bumped on the head.

The stranger kept coming, racing the prairie wind—the same impetuous wind that had whipped Angela's hair into a stringy sculpture of dried mud and feathers. Feeling a sudden rush of anticipation at meeting this stirring essence from the romantic past, Angela pulled her hair back, then wrinkled her nose at its gritty feel. Heaving a sigh, she resigned herself to the fact that the only impression she was going to make today was of a grubby guilty defendant, liable for damages to a pickup truck and fifty-odd traumatized chickens.

The rider was quickly upon them, reining in hard. The stallion's front hooves pawed the sky mere inches from Angela's defunct car. Only when the man bounded to earth with a reckless grace did she realize that her tall-in-the-saddle vision was indeed Tarrant Seaton. The crazy thought that had dashed through her brain hadn't been the result of her head injury, at all. She stared. He looked completely different now—rugged, untamable and totally unlike the polished, impeccable man she'd come to know.

"What's the trouble here?" he asked, striding over to them, his manner as authoritative as his other, executive persona, although he was outfitted in close-fitting jeans and a well-worn black flannel shirt.

"Oh, hello, Mr. Seaton," Mr. Kilgore said, his tone respectful. "This here lady rammed my truck and almost scared my Reds to death."

Tarrant slanted her a curious look. "Are you all right?"

Angela was surprised by his concern, but she nodded.

He moved a step closer. When he lifted his hand to her forehead, she flinched and took a step backward, trying not to be affected by the heady spice-and-leather scent he exuded.

"Dammit, stand still," he demanded. "Let me check that cut."

She lowered her eyes and ducked her head. "It's nothing."

His hand was warm as it smoothed away the muddy, crusted hair. "It's swelling."

She clenched her teeth, but said nothing. The touch of his fingers was sweet torture, and she hated herself for being so affected by it.

His hand was quickly gone and she could hear him walk away. Casting him a sidelong glance, she watched as he went over to examine her car and the pickup for damage.

"Come here, Joe," he called to the farmer.

Angela watched covertly as Tarrant spoke quietly to the farmer. After a few minutes, the farmer shook Tarrant's hand. Angela frowned, confused. It seemed that the two had struck some kind of deal.

The farmer turned to look at Angela, lifted a hand that seemed almost friendly and shouted, "Hope that head's okay, miss." Then he jumped in his truck and drove off.

Angela was so perplexed she couldn't think. Tarrant was beside her before she'd registered the fact that he'd even moved. "It's hard to tell, but I don't think your car sustained much damage. Other than two flat tires, that is. Do you have any spares?"

She shifted her gaze to meet his, still bewildered. "What?"

He smiled, but more with frustration than humor. "I asked if you have any spare tires."

She shook her head.

"Why am I not surprised?" he mused aloud.

"Where did that man go? I didn't even give him my name or address or insurance—"

"Forget about it. He's taken care of."

She stared. "What do you mean? What did you do?" She felt a sudden irritation. Her pride wouldn't allow him to make her a charity case! "I won't have your pity! I can pay my own way, thank you very much!"

"Oh, shut up, Angela," he stated tiredly. "You were working for me at the time of the accident. Morally, it's my responsibility."

"No, it's not!" she retorted. "I refuse to take your charity."

"It's not charity, dammit. Come on. It's getting late and you're wet. You'll catch your death."

"It's eighty degrees out here," she shot back. He had her by the arm and was pulling her away from her car. "Where are you taking me?" she cried, exasperated.

"You can't drive that car."

"But... but I can't go anywhere like this! I'm filthy."

"I noticed."

"You're so gallant!" she choked out as they reached the grazing stallion. "Just what do you expect me to do?"

With his hands at her waist, he hoisted her up. "Slide a leg across the saddle and hold on to the horn."

She yelped in surprise as she was lifted into the air. Frantically she grabbed the saddle horn and did as she was told, retorting, "But I've never ridden a horse."

He mounted, sliding her hips against his thighs. Slipping an arm about her middle, he murmured, "But I have."

He guided the horse toward a path into the nearby wood.

"We're not headed back to the mansion," she protested weakly, her mind focused on the solid feel of this powerful man and the disquieting knowledge that her hips were wedged intimately in his lap.

"You're too dirty to go into the house, and I don't think you'd take kindly to being hosed down by the gardener."

"So...so where are we going?"

"There's a hunter's cabin not far from here. You can clean up there."

She twisted around to eye him dubiously. "What are you doing here, anyway? I thought you'd gone somewhere to look over some property."

He gave her a slight smile. "I am. Once again, you've blundered into my business."

She faced forward, observing tartly, "My brakes went out. Believe me, the last person I wanted to see today was you!"

He chuckled sardonically. "Look around you, Angela. It's getting dark. I'd say your wish has come true."

"My wish? Oh!" Squeezing her eyes shut, she muttered, "Egomaniac..."

He laughed again, and she felt it radiate through her body. Unfortunately, imprisoned against him as she was, there was little Angela could do but endure his amusement at her expense.

CHAPTER EIGHT

ANGELA STOOD UNCERTAINLY in the middle of the neat one-room cabin, feeling increasingly gritty as the mud dried and began to make her skin itch. "Where do I clean up?" she asked, glancing around. On one side of the cabin were two metal beds covered with gray wool blankets pulled military-taut. On the other side, some rough shelves stocked with canned goods stood next to a long expanse of unvarnished counter. Near the counter squatted a heavy oak table and four chairs; a stone fireplace with a wide hearth faced the entry. It had been neatly swept out, and a stack of fresh wood waited in the corner.

When Tarrant didn't answer her immediately, she turned to locate him. He was pulling some rope from a drawer. Curious, she asked, "What's that for? Do you intend to bind and gag me?"

He headed toward the hearth, passing her a wry grin. "It's kind of you to offer, but I don't think that'll be necessary."

She planted filthy fists on her hips. "Ever the humorous—"

"Maggot, I know," he finished for her. "As to your earlier question. There's a creek out back."

Her eyes narrowed, and she wondered what earlier question she might have uttered that had anything to do with the topography of the surrounding landscape. "So what if there's a creek out back?"

He tied one end of the rope to a nail protruding from the unpainted wood wall before looking at her. "You wanted to know where you could bathe...."

Her mouth dropped open. "Do you mean to tell me you expect me to...to..."

He lifted an eyebrow. "What's the matter, Angela? Haven't you ever skinny-dipped?"

Shocked by the question, she snapped her mouth shut, then stuttered, "Well... well, n-not in years."

That made him grin, giving him a thoroughly rakish expression. "And I bet you weren't alone, either."

She felt heat rush up her cheeks at the sensuality of his tone. "I most certainly was. I was six years old! Not all of us live as unrepentant a life-style as you!"

His smile faded and he turned away to tie the other end of the rope to the wall on the opposite side of the fireplace. "Nevertheless, if you want to be clean and dry when you go home, I'm afraid that's your only option."

She surveyed the room. "Well, what can I wear while my clothes are drying?"

He cocked his head toward the cots. "Pull off one of those blankets. It should preserve your modesty adequately enough."

Distrust crept into her voice. "Do you intend to be a gentleman about this and keep your eyes off the creek while I...clean up?"

Without missing a beat, he began to light the fire. Gracing her with only the barest of glances, he remarked coolly, "Do you really think I have to resort to voyeurism to satisfy my erotic urges?"

She blanched at his contemptuous tone. No. Certainly not the Prince of Delights—a man who could hold out his hand and coax any single female within a five state area into his arms. Feeling thoroughly put in her place, she ran to the nearest bed and yanked the wool blanket from the mattress. Then, spinning indignantly on her dirt-caked heel, she retreated outside.

Fifteen minutes later, she dashed back inside, her clothes a dripping mound in her trembling fingers. The water had been freezing, and it had taken all her willpower to peel off her clothes and dunk herself in the icy, churning bath. But she'd done it, and now her skin was tingly and clean, and her dripping hair was free of dirt and feathers.

The blanket was scratchy against her skin, but at least she was less chilled. Once inside, she sputtered, "I-I'm back. Wh-what do I do with my c-clothes?"

He turned from stirring something on the old wood stove, now blazing with heat, and gave her a casual head-to-toe perusal. She shifted from one bare foot to the other, pulling the blanket closer about her. He pointed toward the fireplace. "Toss them across those ropes."

She hurried to do that, but because her fingers were numb and her blanket restricted movement, she kept dropping things. Finally, with a snort of irritation, Tarrant put down his wooden spoon and ambled over to her, taking the wet bundle. "You're quite clever with your hands, aren't you?" he taunted irritably. "Sit on the hearth and get out of the way."

"It's just that I'm c-cold," she retorted as she plunked herself down on the stone. "I'd like to see you do the same thing while you're freezing to death, wearing nothing but a blanket."

"I'm sure you would," he said bitterly. "The surest way to catch a man is to get him undressed so you can cry foul."

She grimaced. "Would you get off that subject? Remember, you brought me here. I didn't ask to come!"

"A misplaced moment of good-Samaritanism. I'll try to watch such impulses in future."

She refused to be cowed by his bullying. Now, she supposed, she was to say a meek thank-you. Well, after his nasty insinuation, he could just whistle for it.

"You're welcome, Miss Meadows," he said casually.

She glared up at him. It embarrassed her when he placed her underwear over the rope, but he made no snide comments; instead, he went about his work matter-of-factly, even though another pair of her Wednesday panties presented a perfect opportunity for a crude remark. She was silently grateful for his decision not to bring up *that* subject again.

Freeing an arm, she ran her fingers through her hair, trying to both dry it and untangle it. For the first time she became aware of the aroma of whatever was bubbling on the stove. "Something smells good," she murmured, not realizing she'd spoken aloud until it was too late. He didn't deserve a compliment, the cad.

"It's canned chili. You're welcome, again," he replied.

She frowned. "Okay, okay. I appreciate everything you've done for me today. I'll admit it and I'll say thank you, if you get off my case about being after you and your money." She caught his stern gaze. "Do we have a truce?"

He watched her silently. For a long moment, the only sound in the room was the crackle and hiss of burning logs. At last, he held out a well-shaped hand. "Deal, Miss Meadows. Truce."

Tentatively, she took it. His fingers were warm, though damp from handling her clothes. As swiftly as she could, she pulled away from his touch and looked down at her bare feet, searching her mind for a safe subject. "I . . . I can't believe I spent the afternoon chasing down chickens. We had a hog farm and I've fallen in mud before, but..."

"You looked like you'd been tarred and feathered."

She shot him a sharp glance, but could see no sarcasm in his face. Though his dark eyes sparkled with humor, his demeanor seemed almost friendly. She had an urge to call him on the remark, but deciding to honor the truce, she let it go.

"How's that bump on your head?"

She tentatively reached up to touch it. It was slightly swollen, and she winced. "A little tender."

He knelt near her, and she could detect again that spicy masculine scent that seemed to cling to him. Brushing the wet hair away from her forehead, he examined her injury by the firelight. He didn't quite frown, but seemed concerned. "We don't have any ice to put on it," he said. "You'll have a bruise, but no black eye this time."

His fingers lingered on her face for an instant longer than she would have thought necessary. Their eyes chanced to meet, hers curious, his enigmatic. Dropping his hand, he stood abruptly. "I'd better check the chili," he stated brusquely, striding away.

"I should be getting home," she called after him. "Scandalmongers would love to get wind of this little scene. We'd make all the gossip columns." She shook her head. "What would such a story do to Eden?"

He glanced over at her from his place before the stove. Somehow, he seemed too big for the small cabin. Shaking his head grimly, he vowed, "No one will find out, because *you* won't tell anyone. I have your promise on that, don't I?"

His tone sounded suspicious again. Hurriedly, she nodded to reassure him. "Believe me, I have no desire for that kind of publicity ever again."

His expression softened slightly. "That's good news. And as for Eden, she trusts me just as I trust her. I'll do nothing to damage that trust."

Their shared kiss in the factory flashed through her mind, and she flinched at the recollection. Apparently Tarrant had the same thought, or he had read hers. "Blast it, Angela," he snapped. "Don't remind me."

She straightened. "I didn't say anything."

He lifted his face to the beamed ceiling. "You irritate the life out of me sometimes. I acted irrationally that night. Have the grace to forget it."

She chewed the inside of her cheek and turned to stare into the dancing fire. It blurred before her. Something that had been singularly revealing to her—something some foolish part of her brain would not let her ignore—meant no more to him than a swat at a pesky insect. And he was asking her to forget it. Trying very hard to prevent her voice from quivering, she said, "For Eden's sake, I will."

"Thank you," he murmured solemnly.

When he didn't say anything else, she was forced to look back at him. He was watching her intently. There was something unexpected in his dusky look, something new. Was it tenderness toward her because she'd shown compassion for Eden? Possibly, but there seemed to be more. Exactly what that more was, she couldn't fathom.

Suddenly his lips twitched into a crooked grin. Even mocking her as it was, his smile lit up his features, stealing Angela's breath. What a devastatingly attractive man he was. She shrank back farther in her scratchy cocoon, distressed by how swiftly and heatedly she'd reacted to his smile. "What are you smirking at?" she demanded, but her voice had come out sounding oddly breathy.

He turned away to take the chili pot off the stove and carry it over to the counter where two bowls waited. "I was just thinking how crazy life can be. I never expected to be cooking you dinner while you were wearing nothing but a blanket.''

Her pride surfaced and she retorted, ''It hasn't exactly been one of my fantasies, either!''

He laughed outright, a sound that filled the cabin with its deep richness. ''Touché, Miss Meadows.'' With a nod, he indicated the table. ''If you're warm enough, why don't we eat over here?''

He placed the bowls on the scarred wood and surprised Angela by holding out a chair for her.

''There's canned apple juice. Would you like it now or for dessert?'' he asked when she was seated.

''Later's fine.'' Fumbling with her blanket, she managed to free one arm, but not without baring a shoulder in the process. The small cabin was toasty, with both the stove blazing and the fire roaring. Having her shoulder exposed wouldn't make her cold. She noted that when Tarrant saw her flesh appear, he averted his eyes, as though the sight of her skin and the snowy rise of a breast bothered him.

They ate in silence. Angela watched Tarrant covertly, thinking of how at home he seemed in this rustic cabin and how adept he'd been on the back of a horse. It seemed that he was as comfortable living in the woods as he was in boardrooms and New York soirees.

He glanced her way, catching her quiet observation of him. Not knowing quite what to say, she mumbled, ''Good chili.''

He smiled that melting smile. ''I'm good at opening cans.''

Working to control a foolish shortness of breath, she had to give him credit for honoring their truce. They'd never spent so much time together without one of them getting angry. She indicated the fire with her spoon, then said, making conversation, "I saw you start that with nothing but a match and a few dry leaves. I thought you needed gas to start a fire."

"For a farm girl, you don't know much." He chuckled. "Your father must not have been very handy."

She felt a stab of regret, but not anger. He was right. Though her father had been a wonderful man in many ways, he wasn't very handy—as with many other things he'd tried, he'd so badly mismanaged the hog farm that he'd lost it. Lowering her gaze, she took another bite without answering.

"That was charming of me," he growled.

She stared at her bowl. Without warning, she felt his hand on hers. "I'm sorry, Angela."

She cast a startled glance at him as he went on, "No matter what our differences might be, I had no right to belittle your father. It was thoughtless."

Unable to drag her hand from beneath the alluring warmth of his, she simply said, "I accept your apology."

His smile this time was tentative and brief. Then, as suddenly as he'd smiled, his features darkened and he stood, muttering, "I'll get that juice."

She sat perfectly still, recalling the touch of his hand, so large and gentle, covering hers. She wasn't even sure that he'd been aware he'd touched her at all. With great resolution, she jerked her hand into her lap, balling it into a fist. She mustn't be affected by this man! She had no right to those feelings—he was engaged to another woman. A perfectly lovely woman. And Angela was nothing more to him than a fleeting good deed.

Once her clothes were dry and she'd changed, he helped her back into the saddle, settling her against him. It was a black night, and she had no idea how either Tarrant or his stallion could pick the way along the wooded path.

He kept one arm securely about her as he guided the horse along. Without wanting to, she relished his solid closeness. She felt like a traitor to Eden, and to herself. But she had to admit that Tarrant wasn't the dyed-in-the-wool womanizer she'd thought him, or the superior snob, either. In a pinch, he could be quite nice, a real gentleman, as he'd proven himself to be at the cabin.

When it had come time for her to change into her dry clothes, he'd excused himself, saying he was going to saddle Cavalier, and had left her to dress in private. He hadn't made a single off-color remark or lewd suggestion. She was amazed by his gallant behavior, and found herself actually enjoying the long trip back to Havenhearth.

She'd expected him to hurry back, and assumed that he was traveling slowly to prevent her from being jounced unmercifully. She decided to thank him for his thoughtfulness. Shifting in the saddle, she said, "I appreciate your considerateness tonight."

She couldn't see his face, but she had the feeling he was surprised by her remark. "Considerateness?"

"I mean walking the horse back, since I'm no horsewoman."

He chuckled, and she felt it all the way to her toes. "It's too dark to go much faster. Unless you don't mind a broken neck."

"Oh, of course," she murmured, feeling deflated and foolish.

After another long silence, when all Angela could hear was the wind, Tarrant said, "I had Joe Kilgore phone for a wrecker to tow your car back to Havenhearth."

"Oh?" She hadn't even thought about her car. Where was her mind? "Thank you."

"I think Chauncey can have the broken brake line fixed tonight, but I doubt if the tires can be delivered before tomorrow morning. You'll have to spend the night."

She felt her heart skip a beat in nervous anticipation. "I . . . I could take a taxi into town."

"And another back to pick up your car? That's starting to sound expensive."

"I'll pay for it," she protested.

He laughed again, causing another delightful tingling sensation to run through her. She wished he would stop inflicting that on her.

"What's funny?" she snapped.

"You're so full of pride, Angela. Be sensible. It's late. You might as well stay. You know we have plenty of room."

She frowned into the night. "You'll tell Lunatic I'm there?"

"He'll be the first to know," Tarrant promised in a whisper that affected Angela in such a subtly intimate way she shivered.

"Are you chilly?" he asked.

"No," she insisted, wishing that they'd galloped headlong home, darkness or no darkness, broken necks or no broken necks. Being this close to the Prince of Delights would be a painfully difficult experience to forget!

RESTLESS, BUT KNOWING the hazards of wandering around the mansion's grounds, Angela pressed the "security" button on her phone and called Alexander to ask if she could recheck some construction detailing in the basement without being arrested or chewed to bits.

When he'd assured her that she would be safe, she pulled the white satin robe on over the matching gown she'd borrowed from Delila and headed downstairs.

It startled her to see lights on when she opened the kitchen door that led to the basement. When she reached the bottom of the stairs, she saw why. Tarrant rounded the corner from one of the storage areas that hadn't yet been cleaned out. He looked endearingly unkempt and dusty. Forgetting that she was in a nightgown, she grinned up at him. "Well, well, don't you look charming," she teased. "What are you supposed to be? A vampire who rises from his dirt-filled coffin to roam the night?"

He smiled, but just barely, as though something was preying on his mind. "I'm glad to see you, Angela."

Her heart leapt stupidly as he took her by the arm, explaining, "I need someone with a small hand."

She was pulled into a storage area. "Can you hear it?" he asked quietly. "That crying sound?"

She did, though it was very weak. Glancing around, she asked, "Where's it coming from?"

He pointed through a narrow gap between stacks of boxes. "Back there. A stray cat managed to get in here and have a litter of kittens on that old sofa. I got back there and rescued them." He indicated a cardboard box containing a calico cat and several squirming newborns of various colors. "But there's one that's fallen down between the springs. My hand's too big to reach it."

Angela gasped. "Oh, the poor thing." Without any further urging, she squeezed through the space and dropped to her knees on the couch. The end cushion was torn, exposing a section of springs. Now the high-pitched mewing sound was clear. Pitiful but clear.

She peered down and could faintly discern something. "I see it," she whispered. Pushing back her lacy sleeve, she dipped her hand inside the springs and very carefully closed her fingers about a tiny, furry being.

"I have it, Tarrant," she cried, gently dislodging the kitten and bringing it up into the light. It was pure white and so small she didn't see how it could possibly survive. Cradling it in her hand, she watched as it flailed and made squeaking sounds.

"Come on, baby, we'll get you to your mother." Carefully she edged back through the rows of stacked boxes. Then, kneeling, she deposited the kitten near its mother's belly.

The mother cat immediately began to lick her kitten tenderly.

When Angela stood, she caught Tarrant's gaze. He was smiling at her. "Thanks," he said.

She shrugged, hoping she didn't blush beneath his soft scrutiny. "I'm glad I could help." Looking down at the expensive robe she was wearing, she grimaced. "Oh, I got your mother's robe filthy."

He picked up the box full of cats. "She's a strong woman. She'll survive the catastrophe."

"Where are you taking them?" Angela asked, following Tarrant into the basement hall.

"Upstairs. It's damp down here."

"What were you doing here in the first place?"

"Storing some old files. With all the work you're doing at the factory, we're short on storage space right now. What were you doing down here?"

"I was going to check on something, but I'll help with the kittens first." As she trailed behind him, she said, "I had no idea you were so fond of cats."

"My affection for animals doesn't make good copy, I suppose, since it rarely appears in the tabloids."

He had climbed the stairs to the kitchen before she told him, "I'd rather have known that about you than some of the things I've read."

He placed his charges in a warm corner beneath a built-in desk, then added a kitchen towel to the box before he straightened and looked at her. "That makes two of us," he said, his expression serious.

She felt it again, that fierce attraction he was able to elicit with a simple direct glance. She turned away, murmuring, "Mind if I give the mother cat a saucer of milk?"

"Go ahead."

She could feel his eyes on her as she moved about the kitchen, getting a saucer and pouring out a bit of evaporated milk and then diluting it with water. "I've heard this is better for cats than whole milk," she began, searching for a harmless subject.

"Whatever," he remarked. "Do you have cats?"

She shook her head, placing the bowl beside the mother. "On the farm we had barn cats. They stayed with the barn when we lost, er, sold the place. I can't have them in the apartment. Landlord's rule. But someday I'd like one."

When she was again standing, he was beside her. "I bet you'll be a good mother."

She was startled into meeting his dark gaze. A lock of hair lay across his brow and a smudge marred his cleft chin. He seemed disarmingly vulnerable, human. Her throat closed, and she didn't know what to say. "I...I bet you'll be a good father," she said after a moment, then winced at her silly comment. What had possessed her to blurt that? She'd never thought of Tarrant Seaton in reference to children until this minute.

He was watching her with amusement in his eyes. "Do you think so?"

She shrugged, embarrassed. "I don't know. I..." She focused her attention on the cat family. The tiny white kitten they'd rescued was suckling contentedly now, as the mother lapped at the milk. She heard purring. "Oh, look, Tarrant, I think the little one's going to be okay."

"I'll save it for you. What do you want to name it?"

She glanced over at his profile as he, too, watched the newborns. He seemed to sense her appraisal and turned toward her. "Why don't we call it Angel?" he suggested.

"Silly name for a boy," she whispered, for some odd reason unable to speak any louder.

"How do you know it's a boy?" he asked, his mouth forming a small smile.

"It's just a guess, but I have a fifty-fifty chance of being right."

"That's an optimistic viewpoint," he observed. "Well, then, what do you want to name your boy?"

"Prince..." It had slipped out without thought. She bit her lip, wondering why she had proposed *that* as a name. He'd think she was naming the cat after him! And she wasn't! The thought was the farthest thing from her mind—wasn't it?

He lifted a curious brow, then nodded. "Prince, it is. Maybe he'll wear the title more easily than I do."

His face was devoid of emotion. Unable to stop herself she asked, "Don't you enjoy being the Prince of Delights?"

He favored her with a cool look. "How could I help it, when it brings me notoriety in the national press and all manner of deluded women in the dark of night?"

Suddenly she could see his side of the problem. After spending the evening with him, she had to admit that some of the news stories she'd read about his prodigal ways seemed overblown. And the night she'd been so rudely manhandled by the guard, she'd been given to understand that a woman sneaking into Havenhearth was not that rare an occurrence. Dropping her gaze to her hands, she murmured, "Rest easy, Tarrant. I'm not one of those deluded women, no matter what you may believe."

There was a drawn-out moment of quiet between them; the only sound in the large kitchen was the cat's purring and the soft mewing of her babies as they scrambled for rations.

"Do you have a boyfriend, Angela?" he asked abruptly.

She stared. "Uh, well, of course, I do," she lied.

"Oh?" He smiled wryly, as though he knew she was lying. "Where do you keep him?"

She was silent.

"You notice I didn't say lover," he accused softly. "Can you guess why I made the distinction?"

Numbly she shook her head.

"My mother once said you were an innocent." He gazed at her thoughtfully before he added, "There are times, like when you were scrambling out from behind those stacks of boxes, streaked with dust, a wide-eyed angel of mercy, that I could almost agree with her. And right now..."

The look in his eyes was neither disdainful nor threatening. His lips curved appealingly, and Angela could feel the rising specter of her desire for him. She tried to back away, but he anticipated her flight, pulling her firmly to him as he lowered his mouth to hers. His lips hovered nearer, and she grew alarmed. He was going to kiss her again. What would she do? What *could* she do? Her legs seemed rooted to the floor, and her arms were frozen against her body.

"Don't kiss me, Tarrant," she pleaded hoarsely.

He smiled almost sadly. "Anything you want..."

When his lips touched hers, she was shocked. In the same breath that he'd promised not to kiss her, he'd placed his mouth tenderly against hers.

"Why...?" she breathed, shaken by the depth of feeling his touch aroused.

"Because you wanted me to," he pointed out. "Don't lie to me."

"But you're..." The horrible word *engaged* stuck in her throat. She couldn't even voice the painful reality. In desperation, she forced movement into her hands, which she pressed forlornly against him.

"Don't fight me, Angela," he insisted softly. "You're a lovely, tempting enigma...."

His lips grazed her mouth with a tenderness completely unlike the powerful, angry passions that had launched the last kiss they'd shared. Tarrant's gentleness tonight was blissful, and against her will she was swept away. Her arms lifted to encircle his broad shoulders, just as his went about her waist, pulling her to his hard body.

She moaned audibly as his knowing fingers trailed along her spine, one hand moving slowly up to massage her neck, sending her pulse racing.

His kiss was honeyed torment, her senses growing more and more charged by his touch, and she knew a longing she had never experienced before, a longing to know Tarrant fully—to be his wife, and the mother of his children. Suddenly Eden's face loomed in her mind. Eden would be the mother of Tarrant's children. Eden Leslie, not Angela Meadows. Through a wounded moan, the other woman's name escaped Angela's lips.

Without warning, he broke away from her and, in one long-legged stride, removed himself from her immediate vicinity. "Damn!" he snarled, dragging his hand through his hair, mussing it even more charmingly. "You must think I'm a cheating snake!"

Still overwhelmed by the lingering feel of his lips on hers, his gentle hands against her body, she could not form a coherent word. Her lashes fluttered nervously down, and she missed the look of self-loathing that crossed his face.

His raw oath brought her gaze back up to clash with his. "Forgive me, Angela. I don't know what it is about you...." He shook his head wearily. "Damn me! You looked so sweet standing there." With regret shading his voice he turned away. "I'm engaged, and I've been a jerk to you *and* to Eden."

His face was etched with such torment that Angela couldn't help but think him gallant and irresistible. Without volition, she almost reached out a trembling hand to stroke his jaw. Instead, she clenched her fists and held them tightly to her chest. His kiss had shaken her so badly she didn't dare touch him, for fear of letting him know the extent of her reaction.

When she didn't say anything, he dropped his stricken gaze to meets hers again, muttering, "I can't blame you for not wanting to speak to me." His eyes ranged distractedly over her body for a long, tense moment. Then his expression grew dark and he asked tightly, "Was it really all my fault? Or are you far from the innocent my mother—" He broke off, his voice rough with an emotion she couldn't define. "Which are you, Angela? A shrewd temptress or the naive innocent you appear to be?" Nostrils flaring in frustration, he laughed, but the sound was mirthless. "On second thought, what does it matter? You're my mother's employee. You mean nothing to me." Determinedly he pivoted around her, muttering, "I'll stay out of your way."

Endless minutes passed after the clipped sound of his footsteps no longer echoed along the hallway. Alone now, and still shaken from his kiss and his accusation, Angela dropped to the floor. Forlorn, she tried to find solace in giving comfort to the mother cat. Stroking its head, she whispered brokenly, "That...that's just fine, Tarrant, because you mean less than nothing to me!" She stopped short, and with utter despair, discovered she was crying.

CHAPTER NINE

THE NEXT MORNING Angela awoke to find her clothes pressed and neatly laid out beside her canopied bed. Once dressed, she went downstairs, wondering if Tarrant would deign to join her for breakfast. She hoped not.

When she reached the grand entryway, he appeared unexpectedly from around a corner, looking impeccable in a tan sports coat and dark taupe pleated slacks. There was no sign of the charmingly mussed cat-savior from the night before, but his dark eyes echoed the same frustration she'd noted when he'd stalked out of the kitchen.

With a grim nod in her direction, he muttered something about an early business meeting, adding that her car was repaired and waiting in the drive.

Though Angela made an attempt at polite thanks, his hasty exit cut her off. His undisguised desire to get away from her distressed her more than it should. Why did she have to feel such inappropriate attraction for a man who didn't like or trust her—a man who was about to be married to someone else?

Just then Angela heard a rustle at the top of the stairs and turned to see Delila standing there, clad in a jade-green lounging coat. The older woman called down sweetly, "Ah, I see you're ready for breakfast, my dear. Allow me to join you in the sun room. It's lovely there at this time of the day."

"Thank you, Mrs. Seaton, but I've troubled you enough," Angela hurriedly excused herself. "I need to be going."

"Well, if you must...." Delila's smile held a touch of melancholy as she added, "Angela, don't let my son upset you. He doesn't mean to be unkind. If I might say a word in his defense, Tarrant's bitterness toward women has been honestly earned." Apparently deciding not to go into detail, Delila dismissed the subject with a shake of her head and a sad laugh. "Forgive an old woman's idle babble." With a graceful flick of her hand, she indicated the door. "Now, scoot. Get on with your young life."

A WEEK LATER, during lunch in their apartment above Angela's shop, Minny withdrew something from one of her voluminous pockets and held it across the rickety table, spread with the makings of egg-salad sandwiches.

"Look at this," she said excitedly, momentarily distracting Angela from a piece she'd been reading in the "Famous Folks" column of the *Daily Press*. It was a brief story about Tarrant Seaton being seen at the opening of a Broadway show last week. The story said he'd gone there to meet his fiancée, Eden Leslie, who was on a buying trip for her trousseau. The accompanying photo showed them arm in arm, smiling fondly at each other. Angela felt a hard lump form in her stomach at the sight of the devoted couple, and she tried to suppress the unhappy feeling. *How stupid!* she chided herself. *For once, you see him depicted in the newspaper as a nice, monogamous man on a night out with his fiancée, and it upsets you? You're a strange case, Angela Meadows! Mind your own business!*

"Mother, did you see this article?" she asked, forgetting that Minny had spoken. "It seems the Prince of Delights is finally settling down. Here he is with Eden—"

"Settling down nothing!" her mother broke in with a disdainful sniff. "Not until he marries you. And he will! I dreamed it, and I have the power," she proclaimed. "Which brings me to what I was saying before, daughter. See what I'm holding?"

Angela glanced up, spotting an exquisite silver pocket watch dangling from her mother's fingers. "Where did you get that?" she asked, taking it from her mother and turning it in her hands. It was obviously an antique, with a delicately engraved likeness of Havenhearth on one side and the initial "S" in swirling script on the other. As she touched a button, the side with the "S" popped open to reveal the face of the watch as well as a miniature sepia photograph of a lovely young Delila Seaton. Frowning with curiosity, Angela gazed across the table at her beaming mother. "Why, this must belong to Mrs. Seaton. Did she drop it here in the shop? If she did, we'd better notify her immediately. She's probably frantic."

Minny shook her head. "No, dear. Delila didn't lose it. I borrowed it."

A shiver of foreboding ran through Angela. "Borrowed?" she repeated weakly.

Minny nodded. "From Delila's bedroom. Yesterday, after I had lunch with her, I saw it lying on her dresser. Belonged to her husband, you know. I wanted to dream on it and find out a little more about the great Noah Seaton. And, daughter, you won't believe what I dreamed! Why, it's so amazing—"

"Mother!" Angela cried. "Don't tell me you took this without permission! Please don't tell me that!"

Minny gave her daughter a disapproving frown. "Why, Angela June Meadows, have you no shame? How could you think such a thing of your mother!"

Angela relaxed measurably. "Well, thank goodness for that. It was lovely of Delila to allow you to borrow it."

Minny stood, brushing crumbs from her lap. "It certainly was, and the minute I tell her about the dream, Delila won't mind a bit. Why, that poor woman has—"

"What are you saying? I thought you said you had permission to borrow the watch!"

Minny took her plate to the sink. "In a way, I did. You see, it simply called out to me—'Minny, Minny, I have things to tell you. Important things!'" She shrugged. "What could I do? Noah Seaton himself gave me permission."

Angela was sitting very erect now. Horrified. She looked down at the watch, hoping desperately that Delila hadn't called the police yet. "Mother, I can't believe this. Thank heaven I have to go out there this afternoon to supervise the installation of a safe in the master bedroom. I'll return it while I'm there."

Minny turned from the sink to face her daughter. "But don't you want to hear the dream?"

Distractedly, Angela cleared the table. "I don't want you to ever mention that watch again. It's probably worth hundreds of dollars, maybe thousands. That's grand theft, you know."

Minny tsk-tsked at her daughter. "Oh, Angela, Delila and I are fast friends. I'd allow her to borrow anything I own without my permission, and I'd never think of calling the police."

"That's all well and good, but we don't own anything worth hundreds of dollars. Delila couldn't get much jail time for borrowing your dog-biscuit earrings or your tin-can jewelry."

Minny laughed. "Darling, you're such a doomsayer. Well, no matter. You return it this afternoon if it makes you feel better. But that dream, you simply must know—"

"*Goodbye*, Mother," she interjected as she grabbed up her briefcase. "Tell Richard I'll be back around five. If there are any emergencies . . ." She paused, correcting herself. "If there are any *more* emergencies, he can reach me at Havenhearth."

AFTER ALEXANDER admitted her with his usual austere grace, she headed for the master bedroom, the pocket watch clutched guiltily in her fist. To her great dismay, she ran into Tarrant—literally—as she dashed along the hall, cannoning into his chest.

"Oh, jeez!" she spat out as her cheeks reddened.

Taking Angela by the arms, he steadied her, then set her away from him. "Looking for me?" came his taunting drawl.

Against her will, she became overpoweringly conscious of his scent. Disliking her reaction to his nearness, she felt impatient to escape, and shrugged out of his hold. "Actually, I was on my way to the master bedroom." Her gaze cautiously met his and was held there.

"The master bedroom?" His brow quirked. "You're very direct today. But I must disillusion you—that isn't my bedroom. It's my mother's."

"I'm perfectly aware of that!" she said, indignant. "I'm here to oversee the installation of her closet safe."

"Oh?" His mouth twitched with wry humor. "My mistake, then. I'll leave you to your work."

She flinched. He'd known why she was there all along and was having fun with her! She had half decided not to even admit that her mother had taken the watch. It had been her plan to make a clean breast of the whole matter to Delila, but since she was out and there was only her arrogant son to confess to, Angela was having second thoughts.

Suddenly he looked dubious. "Why do I suddenly feel like I'm entertaining a felon?"

His astute observation took her off guard, and her indignant pose deserted her. "I...I..." She shifted her guilt-ridden eyes, unable to face him. Holding out her hand, she opened her fingers. "My mother borrowed this to, uh, dream on. I'd like to return it."

His hand brushed hers as he removed the watch from her grasp, and she had to concentrate on ignoring its warming effect.

"I see," he stated. "I'm sure your mother was going to bring it back eventually." The remark was perfectly polite, but left the distinct impression that he didn't believe it for an instant.

She shot him an unrepentant glance. "Naturally! She would *never* steal!"

His frowning scrutiny told her he wasn't convinced.

"I could have just put it back. You would never have known!" she defended herself. "But I chose to be honest with you."

"Commendable," he drawled, his lips twisting sardonically.

Angela was appalled by his cool, disbelieving expression. He didn't have to say it; she knew he thought she and her mother were not only conniving liars but also thieves, however inept. Clearing a lump from her throat, she croaked, "Do you intend to fire me?"

"If you'll recall, Miss Meadows, I didn't hire you."

His words had the feel of a slap. Insulted, she started to march past him, but he placed a halting hand on her wrist. "Aren't you going to tell me what Minny dreamed? I suppose my father blessed our mythical union from his grave?''

She jerked her arm free. "I have no idea what she dreamed. I didn't ask."

"Oh? I'd have thought you'd be happy to announce that the dear departed approve of our predicted marriage—since you can't get the living, breathing groom to fall into step."

"You're a horrible boor!" she flung at him, frustrated at being caught between her mother's crazy prophesies and Tarrant's suspicions.

A long, tense silence stretched between them as Tarrant's gaze searched her face. When at last he spoke, his words were harsh, yet whisper-quiet. "Dammit, Angela, there was a moment a few days ago when I thought we'd gotten past this foolish marriage ploy."

She knew the moment he meant. When they'd looked down at the helpless, newborn kittens, she'd experienced a sweet and unfamiliar tranquillity. She was surprised to discover he'd felt it, too. Unable to withstand the brooding intensity of his eyes, she glanced away. "How's Prince?" she asked in a low voice.

"He's always hungry."

"I don't know when I can take him."

"I realize that."

She thought she noticed a slight softening in his manner and lifted her gaze to meet his. "May I see him later?"

"Whenever you want," he said. "They're in the kitchen."

"Thank you." He seemed irritated, but he also seemed subdued, even bleak, and her foolish heart went out to him. "Tarrant, I'm sorry about this whole mess between you and me. I know you won't believe it, but there never was any marriage ploy. You're engaged, after all. I was hoping, though, that we might become . . . friends.'' The pause before she'd uttered the word "friends" disconcerted her. It was as though she was struggling with the limitations of the word. She shook off the notion. There couldn't be anything between Tarrant and her *but* friendship. If he was willing to allow even that small concession . . .

His deep, wry chuckle startled her. "I wish I had a nickel for every women who's said that to me—just before her trunks showed up on my doorstep."

He had turned her overture of friendship into a joke! It hurt—much more than it should have. Someday she was going to have to figure out why this man had such power over her emotions. But she was too upset to be rational now. Instead, she snapped, "Don't panic! You'll never trip over anything of mine."

He frowned. "Angela, I wasn't—"

"I'm sure you have tons of pithy witticisms left, but I don't care to hear them," she retorted coldly, cutting him off. "And just for the record, Mr. Seaton, I wouldn't have you if you were served to me on a skewer, although the idea is appealing!" She darted past him, hoping he would keep his distance for the remainder of her business there.

For the next three hours, she moved about the mansion checking on work in both the basement and the master suite, all the while trying to ignore a painfully gorgeous man who disliked her intensely, a man with the irritating capacity for showing up everywhere she seemed to go. She could see that finding himself in the same room with her irked Tarrant just as thoroughly as it did Angela. Even so, their paths kept crossing, as though some dark demon was attempting to make them both miserable.

She took a much needed break at four o'clock and visited the kittens. Holding Prince to her cheek, she cooed to him, wishing she could take him home when he was old enough, but knowing her landlord would never permit it. The cook chatted on about how they'd found future homes for all the kittens but one, and that she thought Prince was the sweetest natured among them.

Unlike his namesake, Angela mused. Just as the thought tumbled from her harried brain, in walked the Prince of Delights himself. She knew he saw her immediately, but he ignored her and spoke to the cook. "I'll be going out for dinner, Eva. Mother's eating here, though."

"Yes, sir," the chubby older woman said with a nervous giggle. "I'm planning on making your favorite for tomorrow. Will you be here then?"

Tarrant granted her his most charming smile, and Angela turned away to avoid being affected by it as he assured the woman, "There's no way I'd miss your famous sole amandine, Eva. Count on me."

Surprising Angela, he bit out, "Will you be here tomorrow, Miss Meadows?"

She shook her head, reluctantly making eye contact. "Not for a few days."

His lips twisted enigmatically before he strode from the room. Though she couldn't quite tell if he'd smiled, she decided it was unlikely that he would pine for her in her absence.

Ten minutes later, while heading back to the master suite, Angela heard a commotion on the second-floor landing.

"But Tarrant, *darling!*" a woman screeched. "If you'd only get to know me, you'd realize what a terrible mistake you're making marrying that Eden woman!"

"Madam, please calm yourself," Alexander implored sedately, while he and Tarrant urged a squirming woman down the stairs. "Mr. Seaton and I don't want you to fall."

"I won't go!" the redhead howled, and Angela's mouth dropped in astonishment as she realized it was Marty from the candy factory. She was clad in a short pink nightie and a large black raincoat. It was clear that Tarrant had thrown his own coat across her shoulders to help preserve her modesty for her journey home.

"Marty, you're not thinking clearly," Tarrant was saying. "Don't do this. You're a lovely woman, and you shouldn't make a fool of yourself like this."

"I can't help it," she wailed. "I love you so, Tarrant!"

Angela had to flatten herself against the banister as Tarrant and Alexander went past, half carrying the woman between them. She was sobbing now, trying her best to grab Tarrant even though each man had a strong grip on her upper arms.

"You don't love me," Tarrant insisted calmly. "Please don't try anything like that again. It isn't safe to stow away in a laundry truck."

Angela watched the scene in horrified wonder. She knew Marty had recognized her, for the redhead had turned a hateful countenance on Angela as she'd been hauled past.

"Madam," Alexander soothed, "a taxi has been summoned for you. Chauncey will drive you to the gate and wait with you there. Your fare has been paid."

"No-o-o-o-o," Marty sobbed. "I won't leave you."

The door closed without much sound, effectively blocking out Marty's noisy lamentations.

Tarrant, alone now, turned back toward the stairs before he realized Angela was standing there. He paused, his cool eyes raking her face. "You look surprised," he remarked, almost too calmly, as if he was holding himself in tight control.

She swallowed. "I guess this sort of thing really does happen to you all the time."

A brow arched. "What sort of thing?"

"You know very well what sort of thing—women hiding in the laundry and sneaking into your room."

"Oh, that?" He thrust his hands into his pockets. "Hardly ever—just weekdays and Sundays."

Her lips twitched, forming a tiny incredulous smile, and she felt an odd combination of annoyance and compassion. "What? No Saturdays?"

He lifted one shoulder in elegant dismissal, and she was hard put not to notice the play of muscle beneath his knit shirt. "I believe they attend their 'how to catch a man with money' meetings on Saturdays."

"Oh, they do, do they?" she retorted.

"Aren't you a card-carrying member of the club?"

"I won't dignify that with an answer," she told him, her affable mood disintegrating.

He cocked his head questioningly, giving her a disconcertingly direct look. "Does that mean I should pencil you in for Saturday, then? My bedroom balcony, around six?"

There had been a taunting, yet seductive quality in his words that sent a wave of something like desire sweeping through her. It was so unexpected and unwanted she grew angry with herself. Forcing iciness into her tone, she informed him, "Sure! Pencil me in! And why don't you hold your breath until I show up?" With that, she spun around and dashed up the steps.

When she reached the master suite, she slammed the door, trying to shut out the memory of those tormenting ebony eyes. It did no good.

ANGELA WAS JUST READY to leave the Seaton mansion when Delila entered her bedroom. "I understand you were audience to one of my son's, er, romantic adventures this afternoon," she remarked with a smile.

Angela felt her cheeks go hot. "Yes. It was appalling. How did you know about it?"

Setting her suede bag down on a Chippendale commode, she said, "Alexander's lapel is torn. He explained how it happened." She absently patted her cap of champagne-colored hair, "He goes through more uniforms that way, poor man. We should give him combat pay."

Delila sat down in an English rosewood chair covered in a deep-wine velvet that echoed one of the rich colors in the needlepoint rug. The same dark red swathed the windows and her ornate Renaissance Revival bed.

Slipping off her high heels, Delila sighed. "This type of silliness has been happening since Tarrant was sixteen." She smiled dispiritedly, shaking her head. "He *is* quite good-looking, don't you think?"

Angela clenched her fists and mumbled, "I suppose."

Delila laughed. "I'm sorry, my dear. Forgive a mother's pride. It's just that his looks coupled with his fortune... Well, it does make for a few inconveniences from time to time. I'll certainly be thankful when Tarrant marries. Perhaps these irrational women will leave him alone."

"I would think so," Angela offered unenthusiastically. "Uh, Mrs. Seaton, would you care to see how your closet is coming along?" she asked, struggling to change the subject.

"Oh, certainly," Delila said. "But first, let me give you something." She stood and went to the commode, where she retrieved a creamy envelope. Returning, she offered it to Angela. "This is an invitation to a ball I'm holding to celebrate Tarrant and Eden's engagement. I want you and Minny to come."

Angela took the envelope gingerly, as though it held a ticking bomb instead of an engraved invitation. The last place on earth she wanted to be was at a ball celebrating

Tarrant's upcoming wedding. "I don't think we can," she began, but grimaced when she realized she didn't know the date yet.

"Oh? How can you be sure?"

Caught in her lie, Angela could only ask, "I, uh, when is it?"

"A week from Saturday. Minny has already assured me that your calendar is clear."

Trapped, Angela nodded forlornly. "Well, then, I suppose... we'd love to come."

Delila smiled. "That's wonderful. Oh, and it's formal." Her expression altered slightly to concern. "Will there be a problem with that?"

Angela felt a stab of pride, assuring her quickly, "Not at all." But in truth, she had no idea what she would do about a dress.

Delila was walking toward the huge closet. "I'll tell you what—I'll have my dressmaker drop by your store. She was telling me just the other day that she's unfortunately overbought some buttercup-yellow silk. I imagine she could create a gown for practically nothing. She's been begging me for weeks to have something made from it, but I look ghastly in yellow."

Angela wasn't buying this. It was charity, pure and simple. "No, thank you, Mrs. Seaton—"

Delila turned back, interrupting. "The closet looks wonderful. I can't even tell there's a safe in there. Come here, my dear," she beckoned. "Show me how to open it."

As Angela came forward to do her bidding, Delila commented casually, "I think something slim would be nice, don't you?"

"Slim?"

"Your dress."

"Oh, please, I can't let you do it."

Delila patted her hand. "Don't deny me this. Once, long ago, Noah Seaton was kind to me when I was starting out in business. I'd like to think I was paying back that kindness by helping others who are struggling to get started. You'll make wonderful contacts at the party, my dear. Allow me to help a little with your gown."

Angela looked away, embarrassed. She didn't know what to do. But finally she managed a compromise. "If you insist. However, I must insist on subtracting the cost from my bill."

"Done."

"How will I know how much to deduct?"

"I'd guess about five...rather, fifty dollars. As I said, she has so much of that buttercup color, she'll be thrilled to be rid of it."

Angela doubted fifty dollars would even begin to pay for the labor, but she didn't know how to call Delila Seaton a bold-faced liar. After all, she *was* Delila's employee. At a loss, Angela offered a weak smile. "What can I say? Thank you, Mrs. Seaton."

Delila beamed, nodding. "Wonderful. I'll have Madame Goida give you a call for consultation and fitting."

Her emotions bordering on hysteria, Angela couldn't help but smile at the absurdity of it all. A consultation and fitting? Madam Goida? Fifty dollars indeed! "That will be fine," she agreed, mentally deducting five hundred dollars from her bill. This simple slim dress didn't sound as though it was going to be any bargain-basement steal for Delila, no matter what she said. Angela hoped the dress would hold up for fifty years, so she could get her money's worth out of it!

As she and Delila went into the closet and Angela was explaining the workings of the secret panel where the safe was hidden, her mind drifted traitorously to a vision of

Tarrant Seaton, tall and powerfully elegant in a tuxedo, his loving smile trained on sweet, pale Eden. She chewed the inside of her cheek, hoping she and Minny could make a brief appearance, maybe have a cup of punch and then get out of there. Angela had never been to a gala ball in her life, but she had a feeling *this* ball would not be a memory she would dwell on fondly in her old age.

CHAPTER TEN

ANGELA WAS MORTIFIED when she braked her old car and it made a nightmarish screech, drawing the startled attention of elegantly clad party-goers nearby. A maroon-garbed attendant, one of the dozen or so hired to park cars for the Seaton engagement ball, bounded over to her car. He managed to get her door open after a few minutes of heroic effort. Then he took her arm, assisting her from the car. "I'll park it for you, ma'am."

When she tried to hand him a tip, he refused, flicking a look at her car. "We're not allowed to accept tips, ma'am," he assured her with a grin, but she had a sinking feeling they'd been ordered not to accept a tip from a certain, destitute-looking pair of women driving a poor excuse for transportation. But she had other, more pressing things on her mind, so she decided to let it go.

Giving him a parting nod, she joined her mother, who'd been helped out by yet another young attendant.

Straightening her handmade, tie-dyed gown, Minny exclaimed, "My, my, what a fancy party. Looks like there must be a hundred cars here."

Angela scanned the sea of expensive automobiles already parked along the circular drive and in a roped-off area of the grounds. "Maybe they wouldn't notice if we didn't show up at all."

Minny touched her daughter's arm. "Now, now. Where's your business spunk? You must meet and mingle, sweetie. This is your big chance to get to know people who can make your shop a household word.''

Angela had to admit her mother was talking sense. With a sigh, she said, ''Okay, but watch for my signal. A glass of punch, one turn among the guests, and we're out of here.''

''What's your signal again?'' Minny asked.

''I'll probably just say, 'Let's go, Mother.' ''

Minny pooh-poohed the idea. ''Make it more exciting than that. Why don't you hoot like an owl?''

Angela laughed at the joke, feeling some of the tension leave her body. ''You're very funny.'' Taking Minny's arm, she headed for the brightly lit entry, fighting a growing feeling of dismay. She didn't want to be here. But there had been no way out of it. Once Minny had received the invitation, she'd spoken of nothing else. She'd spent all week making the puff-sleeved creation she had on. Besides, Angela was now the proud owner of a strappy, clingy, buttercup-yellow Madame Goida gown. A frugal person, she decided she'd better get at least one wearing out of it.

Angela had to admit, even if only to herself, that she felt quite elegant in the dress. She'd been surprised by how lovely it was. At first, she'd felt as though she was wearing a long, flared slip, but her mother and Madame Goida had raved about how chic she looked. And the color did set off the green in her eyes and her golden skin tone. The fake topaz earrings her mother had bought at a garage sale were a perfect match. With Angela's dark hair swept back behind her ears, the costume jewelry was shown off, sparkling as brightly as the real thing.

Inside the mansion, Alexander took Angela's buttercup-yellow wrap and led them through the double doors to the left of the entry hall. Her job hadn't required her to go into the ballroom, so it made an immediate and dramatic impression with its cathedral ceiling and wall of windows, swathed in crimson drapes. The floor was a glowing polished wood, the remaining walls a rich, dark wood and the high white ceiling rimmed with a lavish neoclassical cornice. Massive crystal chandeliers sparkled and glinted, and Angela's overall impression was one of grandeur and glittering light. The huge room teemed with sleekly perfect people. An orchestra at the far end was playing something she recognized as Russian, from the Romantic period. The melody was both haunting and enchanting, but it didn't ease her trepidation.

"Look, sweetie," Minny whispered, tugging on Angela's arm. "There's Tarrant, over there beside the yummy-looking refreshment table. Let's go talk to him."

"No," Angela fairly hissed. "I don't plan to speak to him at all. I came here strictly to make business contacts, and Tarrant is not anyone I care to do business with ever again!"

Minny shook her head at her daughter. "Well, I'm going. You do what you must. But I swear, I don't know where you get your stubborn streak."

Before Angela could stop her, Minny was scurrying away, her tin jewelry clanking loudly, her red-and-blue frock billowing in her wake. Angela hesitantly allowed her gaze to trail over Tarrant, so tall, with such impressive shoulders. He was devastating in his white tuxedo as he talked with an admiring group, one arm casually draped about Eden's shoulders.

She was more beautiful than Angela had ever seen her, with her pale hair pulled up in a smooth twist, entwined artfully with pink roses. Eden's dress was slender, high-necked and fashioned of pink lace. She looked like a Victorian princess. Tarrant and Eden were truly the perfect couple.

Angela averted her eyes. She couldn't bear to see his face when he was accosted by Minny. Nevertheless, she found her glance trained on him seconds later, just as Minny confronted him with an airy greeting.

Angela watched, immobile, as her mother gestured and postured in animated conversation. Tarrant's attention was focused on Minny, his expression polite if a bit grim. When Minny lifted a hand in Angela's direction, his gaze followed and he stared for a moment as some dark emotion flitted across his face. Then he abruptly turned away.

Feeling the sting of his disdain, Angela pivoted in the opposite direction, bent on forcing her mind to the reason she was there—business contacts. Luckily, Delila drifted up, wearing an exquisite champagne-colored gown of antique satin. Taking Angela in hand, she presented her to her friends, and Angela did her best to blot out the realization that Tarrant clearly hadn't known she and her mother had been invited!

TARRANT WAS DANCING, holding Eden loosely within his embrace. His face was closed in a thoughtful frown.

"Tarrant? Did you hear me?" Eden asked.

Pulled from his thoughts, he smiled down at her. "I'm sorry, what did you say?"

She gave him a concerned look. "You've hardly heard a word I've said all evening. And you seem awfully distracted. What is it? Is something wrong?"

"It's nothing," he assured her softly. "Mother invited an employee of hers to the party tonight. The woman annoys me. That's all."

"What woman?" Eden asked curiously.

"You met her at dinner a few weeks ago. Angela Meadows. Her mother was there, too."

Eden giggled. "Ah, the woman who put out the strawberries flambe?"

Tarrant grunted out a short laugh. "Yes. Her daughter, Angela, is no less maddening."

"Isn't that her with Ron?" Eden indicated a couple dancing near the windows.

Tarrant turned to see Angela clasped in the embrace of one of his unmarried friends. "It appears to be," he observed dryly.

"My, she looks lovely, doesn't she?"

Tarrant flicked a narrowed glance over Angela, but said nothing.

"Ron seems completely enamored of her," Eden went on, smiling. "She's making quite an impression on Kansas's most eligible men."

"That's a great weight off my mind," he muttered, his lips thinning.

"Wasn't that her mother who came up to us in the restaurant and told you you'd marry her daughter?"

"Yes." Tarrant groaned. "Troublesome women. Unfortunately, Mother seems to like their company."

Eden patted his shoulder as they swayed to a sultry Johnny Mathis classic. "Tarrant, I've never known you to react this way to an employee." Her brow puckered. "Usually you have more patience about such things."

Without comment, Tarrant flashed Angela and her beaming partner one last look, then he swirled Eden away.

ANGELA AND HER MOTHER had been at the party for more than an hour, and for all the good it would've done her in trying to get Minny to leave, Angela might as well have hooted and flapped her arms—maybe even laid a few dozen eggs. Minny was paying no attention.

Angela didn't have the heart to be too angry with her mother. It was plain that Minny had never enjoyed herself so much in her life. She'd managed to dance every dance with one portly, tuxedo-clad gentleman or another, and Angela, even in her need to get away, wouldn't be responsible for cutting short her mother's fun.

Angela had escaped very few dances herself. Now, catching sight of several young men heading in her direction, she hurriedly slipped through a patio door. More to flee Tarrant's glowering presence than the pursuit of the nice bachelors, she decided to wander alone in the shadowy garden. The guests had spilled out onto the terrace and lingered, laughing and talking, about the glistening pool. Angela retreated past the pool to the area beyond, with its profusion of ornamental fruit trees, rare shrubs and several huge, imported boulders.

As a whole, the garden exuded a feeling of untamed romanticism, well-suited to its prairie existence. She roamed farther from the house, passing another granite monolith, marveling at what it must have cost to haul that one majestic stone, nearly ten feet in height and six feet in width, to this mid-Kansas estate. The towering granite was surrounded by a border of perennials, which surged along its rough surface in an intriguing mix of textures and colors. Amid the beauty of nature, Angela found herself suddenly less agitated, and she took a deep, relaxing breath.

Beyond the winding flagstone path stood a magnificent oak, its branches spreading out regally, and then arching back almost to earth. Thinking the limbs might serve as a peaceful, private refuge, she headed toward the tree.

Soft strains of music drifted around her. The orchestra was playing something she recognized from her mother's collection of Perry Como albums, a seductive old ballad called "I've Got You Under My Skin." Her mutinous brain envisioned Tarrant holding Eden on the dance floor. More than once she'd chanced to snag his glance, and he'd scowled at her, making no effort to hide his annoyance. She shook her head, trying to crush out all thoughts of him.

The manicured lawn was damp against her bare toes, and it felt good, clean, lifting her spirits. Throwing caution to the wind, she leaned down and slipped off her high-heeled sandals. Enjoying the damp of the lawn, she shuffled happily out to the oak. She ran her fingers along the rough bark of a low branch as she ducked under the sheltering limbs. Reaching the trunk, she hoisted herself into a waist-high fork, allowing her bare feet to swing free in the cool night breeze.

She smiled, reliving the innocence of childhood. Her silk gown glimmered in the moonlight, and she realized that, though she might feel like a little girl, she was dressed more like a movie star in a glitzy motion picture, maybe an old-fashioned musical. "Now would be the time for the handsome leading man to take me in his arms and tell me how devastatingly beautiful I am," she mused aloud.

"You're very lovely tonight," came a deep, disembodied voice.

Angela's heart almost leapt from her chest. Before she could gather her wits enough to cut and run, Tarrant Seaton strolled from behind the massive trunk, looking even more imposing than usual. He seemed faintly luminous in his white tux, leaving Angela oddly breathless. "I had no idea anyone was here!" she cried.

He reached over his head and took hold of a branch with both hands, but his eyes were intent on her. "Are you trying to get me to believe you didn't follow me out here?" he asked.

She jumped the short distance to the ground and glared up at him. "Oh, sure, I followed you! And I made that stupid little speech on purpose, to humiliate myself, because I *treasure* these moments we share when you ridicule me!"

He was standing indolently, one hip propped against the trunk. Softly he countered, "Do you consider a man saying you look lovely to be ridicule?"

"I, well..." There was a painful shallowness to her breathing, and a tight ache in the pit of her stomach. She could sense tension between them, and was sure Tarrant felt it, too. Of all the places for a person to wander on this vast estate, how in the world had they both ended up here? She had the irrational thought that she'd been led to the tree by some power stronger than her own will. Ridiculous! Her mother's craziness must be rubbing off.

Wishing to avoid his intense scrutiny, she tried to look away. But she couldn't. There was suddenly a hint of torment in his eyes, and it pulled her, held her, touched her heart. She felt herself drawn to him, and stepped quickly back for fear she would do something stupid—like reach out for him. With her retreating step, she found herself caught against the tree trunk, as trapped as a rabbit in a hunter's sights.

Angela heard a low curse and realized it came from Tarrant. Moving toward her, he took her into his arms and kissed her. As his lips devoured hers, Angela fought her desire for this totally inappropriate man. She refused to allow herself even to wonder how and when she'd fallen in love with him, though the insidious truth hovered in her brain. How could she be such an idiot? He was in love with Eden!

Why, then, was he kissing her, holding her in his powerful embrace? He probably didn't believe her when she'd said she hadn't followed him, and he was humbling her, showing his contempt for her.

Struggling to regain her sanity and her flagging self-respect, she strained away from him, crying breathlessly, "You love Eden! How dare you kiss me! You're not being fair to either of us!" The last came out on a broken sob, the feel of his lips still lingering cruelly on her mouth.

His head snapped back as though he'd been slapped, and his eyes flashed with heated emotion. "Fair?" he scoffed. "You're a fine one to use that word. And love?" With a short, contemptuous laugh, he declared, "I don't believe in it. Rationality is the key to a solid relationship. Not some nebulous, fleeting emotion."

Angela was stunned, unsure she'd heard him right. "Are . . . are you saying you don't love Eden?"

"My reasons for marrying any woman are my business, Miss Meadows, not yours," he answered coldly. "If you'll recall, your maneuverings toward matrimony have been far less noble than anything either Eden or I could conceive."

Angela was shocked that he saw her in such a villainous role. With nerves tattered beyond control, she let her arm fly, slapping him hard across the face. As she stumbled toward the house, dismay overwhelmed her, for her body still tingled from the impact of his careless, taunting kiss.

MINNY STUFFED HER CURLERS beneath her hair net and watched as Angela climbed into her twin bed and lay with her back to her mother.

"Sweetie?" Minny asked. "You haven't said a word since we left the party. What's wrong?"

"Nothing."

"You and Tarrant had a lovers' spat," she remarked judiciously.

Angela turned over to look wearily at her mother. "We couldn't possibly have a lovers' spat. He hates me, and I'm . . . I don't like him, either."

Minny sighed. "Did I or did I not see you come in from the garden only moments before Tarrant did? And did both of you not have the same long, stubborn faces?"

Angela shrugged helplessly. "We had words, yes."

"There, you see? I knew you two had had a spat," she stated with a confident nod. "Now, tell me what it was all about. I'm sure it's nothing."

Lowering her eyes, fighting tears, she asked, "Nothing? Mother, Tarrant's getting married in a week—to a woman he doesn't even love. He says marriage should be a rational decision, not based on some . . . some nebulous emotion. Good Lord, he's marrying Eden the way he'd merge with another company."

"That makes sense."

Aghast, Angela jerked up on one elbow and stared. "Treating marriage like a merger makes sense?" she asked incredulously. "It's terrible! It's . . . it's cold-blooded."

"Sweetie, you misunderstand me," Minny admonished. "I mean it makes sense when you consider the dream I had. Remember I told you I dreamed on Noah Seaton's watch?"

Angela eyed heaven unhappily. "How could I forget that watch?"

"Well, I wouldn't know that, daughter," her mother remarked with a concerned note in her voice. "Maybe if you squeeze your eyes closed really tight—"

"Never mind." Harried and dejected, Angela prompted, "So, what did you dream, anyway?"

"Oh, it was quite amazing, really. My dream revealed that Delila connived to marry Noah because she was pregnant with another man's child." Minny looked at her daughter expectantly. "Tarrant Seaton isn't really Noah Seaton's son!"

Angela's mouth fell open. "Mother, you must be wrong!"

Minny shook her head so vehemently her curlers made a rattling sound. "I'm right. Delila, the dear, confided some of this to me. I can't recall quite what she said and what I dreamed, but that's not important, is it? Now where was I? Oh, yes, my dream told me that Noah knew about the baby, but he never told Delila he knew because he loved her so much it didn't matter. Now, that part about him loving her I deduced from what she told me—about how sweetly he treated her and, er, no, I definitely dreamed it. I think. Anyway, I'm sure Noah loved them both, and he always wished Delila had loved him in return. She really did love him, you know. I can see it in everything she says about him. But I'm not sure she realizes it herself. Poor dear. She's got so much money, yet she's so sad. So full of unnecessary guilt."

Angela was thunderstruck as she listened to her mother's ramblings. Apparently Delila had told Minny things she hadn't told another soul. Why she had chosen her mother to confide in was a mystery, but it was obvious she had. Unfortunately, but not unexpectedly, it was also obvious that Minny was giving her dreams credence they didn't deserve. "Mother?" she asked. "When did Delila talk to you about all this?"

"Oh, the first time was a week or two after I burned my jumpsuit. Remember that dream I had about the lion and the dill pickles? Well, it seems I startled her with my prophetic abilities." She stopped and smiled smugly. "I did get a few of the facts a bit backward, though," she amended with an impish shrug. "It seems that the sailor riding the lion into the sea was actually a sailor named Jack Lyon, who'd fathered her child and then gone back to sea, leaving her pregnant and alone. Horrible man. And the dill pickle thing—'' she stopped to chuckle ''—well, I do feel a little silly about that mistake. You see, this Lyon person called Delila 'Dilly'—you know, like in dill pickles?'' She eyed her daughter with haughty superiority. ''Never doubt my powers again, daughter! I have so much power it frightens even me.''

''It's frightened me for years,'' Angela mumbled wryly.

''What's that, sweetie?''

''Nothing.'' She rubbed the back of her neck, baffled. ''Let me see if I have this straight. Do you mean to tell me your dill-pickle dream actually has some basis in reality?''

Minny harrumphed with disgust. ''Haven't you been listening? A *sailor* named Jack *Lyon* was Tarrant's father. He called Delila *Dilly* and—''

''My heavens!'' Angela gasped as she realized the dream's implications. ''And this Jack Lyon left Delila and went back to sea....'' Angela could never forget how crazy her mother's dream had sounded—a sailor riding a lion into the sea, and the ludicrous bit about a poor pickle harvest. But oddly enough, there were some undeniable similarities between Delila's life and that nutty dream.

Could it be that her mother did have minimal, if somewhat twisted, second sight? Angela shook her head in amazement. Apparently Minny's semicorrect dream had opened up long-blocked floodgates for Delila, and once they were opened, she had chosen to confide the rest of the story to Minny. Life could certainly be strange. ''My goodness, Mother, I simply can't believe it!'' she breathed in awe.

''At last, sweetie!'' Minny exclaimed, clasping her hands together. ''I think you've seen the cosmic wonder of it all.''

Angela studied her mother closely, unable to completely relinquish her skepticism. "Tell me exactly, Mother, when did Delila do all this... this talking?"

"One afternoon when we were sitting in the sun by the pool. A lovely warm afternoon. She reminded me about my dilly dream and told me how marvelous my power was." Minny preened, patting her hair net with a theatrical flourish. "Delila said I'd brought a lot of memories back, and they made her want to get some things off her chest—that's how she put it—to someone with a sympathetic heart." Minny smiled dreamily. "She thinks I have a sympathetic heart." Sighing contentedly, she went on, "We had a fine chat, until, silly me, I fell asleep. I'm afraid she hasn't had many real friends—you know, people she could talk to. I was happy to listen."

"You say you fell asleep while she was talking to you?"

Minny appeared abashed. "It was so peaceful and warm, and Delila's voice is so soothing."

"Mother," Angel began as kindly as her fractured mood would allow, "don't you see, you didn't dream anything on Noah's watch—I mean nothing beyond what you'd heard when you were drifting off to sleep that afternoon by the pool. Delila told you everything except that first lion-dill-pickle thing."

Minny looked at Angela with annoyance. "Don't be such a sour grape, daughter. I know what I dream and what I don't. Anyway, back to your lovers' spat, don't you see why Tarrant is going to marry Eden even though he doesn't love her? Delila felt guilty about fooling Noah, so she taught her son that marriage should be a partnership, or some such drivel. I'm all muddled about that." She screwed up her face in thought. "I'll try to dream about that problem tonight. That'll clear things right up."

"But mother, don't you understand..." Angela trailed off. What good would it do to argue? Minny would never acknowledge that she didn't dream any of the things that actually made any sense about Delila and Jack Lyon or her marrying Noah to give Tarrant a name. It was curious that Minny had somehow been sensitive enough to get the lion and the dill parts at all—however mixed-up. Still, Minny was far from being clairvoyant! Too bad she would never admit it, even to herself.

Exhaling heavily, Angela said, "Switch off the light, will you, Mother?" Flipping over in her bed, she thought about everything Minny had divulged. Could it really be that Delila's ongoing guilt about deceiving Noah had caused her to pass on this "partnership marriage" philosophy to Tarrant? It was impossible, wasn't it? On a sudden thought, she turned back, cautioning, "Mother, you mustn't breathe a word of this to anyone. Prophetic or not, it would be devastating for both Delila and Tarrant if the story got out."

"*Well!*" Minny groused as she turned off the lamp. "First, it certainly *is* prophetic. Remember, I have the power! And second, do you think I'd do anything to upset *my* best friend and *your* future husband?"

Angela grimaced and closed her eyes, not knowing quite how to answer that.

THE NIGHT BEFORE the wedding, Angela realized she'd left her new calculator at the Seaton mansion. Knowing it was the evening of the wedding-rehearsal dinner, she thought she could safely return there without running into the Prince of Delights. The paper had announced that the dinner would be miles away at a Wichita country club.

She'd heard from gossip circulating at the Delila's Delights factory that Tarrant had been in a foul mood all week, and employees had taken to hiding when he thundered onto the premises. They couldn't understand why their great leader was so angry about everything lately— the company stock was continuing to rise on the New York exchange, his newest factory in Munich was doing well, and he was marrying the most beautiful woman in the state. What was his problem? the employees had asked each other as they scurried to stay out of his way. Angela certainly couldn't answer that. Though she didn't gossip, she mused that it was merely his true, tyrannical self finally rearing its ugly head.

Another bit of news from the company grapevine made her smile in spite of herself. It seemed that Marty had recently met a cabdriver named Bud who was an up-and-coming rodeo star. Cracked ribs had put him temporarily out of commission for bronc riding but not for courting. And it appeared that the redhead had fallen totally and completely in love with Bud the cabdriver. Considering the time frame, Angela knew it had to be the very same cabdriver who'd taken Marty home from Tarrant's that awful night not so long ago. Angela shook her head. Fate certainly loved a good twist!

Alexander opened the door, disrupting Angela's musings, and ushered her into Havenhearth with a reserved, "Nice to see you this evening, Miss Meadows."

She smiled at him, because she liked the man even though he worked for a nasty-tempered tyrant. "Nice to see you, too. Alexander. I left my calculator in the basement, and I'm going to need it in the morn—"

The soft thud of footsteps on the carpeted staircase halted her words, and she looked up fearfully to see Tarrant loping toward her, boldly attractive in a black tuxedo. When he saw her, he stopped and eyed her coolly.

"Good evening, Miss Meadows." He turned to Alexander. "You may go. I'll handle this."

Alexander seemed to disappear. Angela's attention was so riveted on the aloof elegance of the man on the stairs that she simply didn't notice the butler's exit.

Tarrant strolled the rest of the way down the stairs to stand before her. "To what do we owe this honor?" he asked sarcastically.

"I . . . I left my calculator in the basement."

He nodded without warmth. "A true emergency."

She bristled defensively. "It is if it's your only one. Of course, you'd have no idea about such things," she admonished. "You've probably never owned just one of anything!"

His nostrils flared, and Angela realized she'd hit a nerve.

"Do you mind if I go fetch it?" she asked.

"Here it is," Alexander interjected, appearing again as if by magic. After handing it to Angela and quietly accepting her thanks, he left as unobtrusively as he'd arrived.

"If that's all," Tarrant said, dismissing her as he turned to head back up the stairs.

Lifting a haughty chin, she called, "I was hoping, as long as I'm here, to remeasure your closet. Our Kansas City custom module supplier had a computer problem and lost some data. . . ."

He pivoted around, his expression harried. "Of course, of course! Do whatever you have to do!" he growled. "Hell, Angela, why must you be everywhere I am—my factory, my home, my dreams—?" As though horrified by his own revelation, he cut his words short. His tone sharp, he demanded, "Blast it, why can't you get the hell out of my life?"

Stunned wordless by his hostility, she spun on her heel and fled outside, leaving the double doors gaping in her wake.

A crash of thunder made Tarrant aware that a rainstorm was hammering the landscape full force. Frowning, he strode to the door to stare after her as she escaped into the midst of the maelstrom. "Nice work, idiot," he said to himself. Jerking a frustrated hand through his hair, he shouted, "Angela, you can't drive in this! Come back!"

A flash of lightning illuminated the drive, allowing him to see her struggle with the hood of her car, shoving at it, fighting the rain and wind to get it open. She was having very little luck at anything but getting soaked to the skin.

"Damn!" he growled. Yanking up his tuxedo collar, he headed out into the storm.

CHAPTER ELEVEN

IT HAD TAKEN ANGELA only a few seconds behind the wheel to determine that something was dreadfully wrong with her car. When she turned the key, nothing happened. "Why now?" she moaned. She would have given anything to make a swift getaway.

She vowed she would absolutely not go back into that mansion and ask for help. She would die of pneumonia first! Tarrant thought she made excuses to come out there and be around him! Of course, many women did—she'd seen the evidence of that. But Angela Meadows was *not* one of those women!

Slamming out of her car, she fought the strong, wind-swept rain to get to the front of the car and grapple with the hood. She wasn't sure if she could tell anything by looking at the engine, but action was better than doing nothing, and her only other options were to trudge home in the middle of a rainstorm or go back and admit defeat. Neither choice was very palatable.

Staring down at her car's decrepit old engine, Angela stifled a miserable sob. She couldn't get Tarrant's last words from her mind: "Why can't you get the hell out of my life!"

Determinedly, she reached in to wiggle wires, sweeping rain from her face as best she could. Nothing seemed particularly loose, but she was no expert.

A hand on her arm surprised her as Tarrant's deep voice growled, ''Angela, if your car has broken down, you can't fix it in this weather! Come back inside.''

Still smarting from his earlier statement, she jerked free of his grasp. ''Don't order me around, Mr. Seaton.''

His expression was hard, but held no malice; he seemed more regretful than angry. For the first time she realized he was standing there in his tuxedo, and it was fast becoming ruined. She faced him squarely, not hiding her indignation. ''Don't spoil your clothes. Go back to the house,'' she insisted. ''I wouldn't want you to think I was finding puny excuses to be near you!''

Because of the deafening storm and the darkness, she wasn't sure if she'd seen or merely imagined the raw vulnerability in his eyes. His perfect hair was drenched and falling in dark curls across his wide brow. With less harshness, he persisted, ''Angela, don't be stubborn. If I apologize—''

''We mustn't have you doing that!'' she broke in. ''An apology implies a wrongdoing, and everyone *knows* the Prince of Delights is perfect—especially the Prince himself!''

His face was beautiful, even marred by distress. She felt drawn to him again, and grew angry with herself for her weakness. Her stand of defiance was crumbling fast, and she knew she'd better get away from him, or he would read the awful truth in her eyes. Spinning abruptly, she marched off down the circular drive. Her pride forced her to shout back, ''I'll walk home. Feel free to charge me for overnight parking!''

With an unsettling abruptness, the ground was swept from beneath her feet. Crying out, she grabbed for the first solid object she could find. It turned out to be Tarrant's shoulder. He'd lifted her bodily and was carrying her back into the house, shouting over the wind and rain, "You're the most pigheaded woman I've ever had the misfortune to encounter!"

"You're a fine one to call me names! Let me go this instant!" she yelled, undermining her demand by continuing to hug his neck.

"Don't tempt me," he warned near her ear.

Suddenly the rain was no longer pelting them, and they were enveloped in light. Angela peered about her and realized Tarrant had made quick work of the steps and had carted her inside. She glanced over his shoulder to look out at the storm. It was getting worse.

When her gaze chanced to lift to Tarrant's face, she was again stunned by the rainwashed beauty there. His dark curls shone like black patent leather. Water sparkled on his lashes and dripped freely from the cleft in his chin. He was frowning at her, but not with annoyance; instead, he looked somber and watchful.

She'd been squirming in his arms the whole way back to shelter, but his expression halted any further desire to fight him. An odd warmth rushed from the pit of her stomach, and for a moment she was barely aware that her clothes were cold and soaked. Weakly she made one last-ditch effort to save herself, whispering, "Tarrant, please put me down. I'll wait by the door until the rain dies away."

"What about your dead car?"

How had she managed to forget about her car? She swallowed nervously, wishing her pulse would stop racing. "I'll call a cab."

He said nothing, and his silent, intent observation was disconcerting. She couldn't tell if he was going to shout at her again or— She shook off a foolish thought. For a crazy instant, she'd thought he wanted to kiss her.

"Dammit, Angela..." She winced. He was going to shout. But then he said in a low, pained voice, "I'm sorry about treating you so shabbily. I was vindictive and unfair. Can you forgive me?"

She could hardly believe her ears. "I—I... Of course. I heard you've been under terrific pressure lately."

A dark brow arched. "You heard that?"

She nodded, wishing she weren't so near him. His strong heartbeat felt as though it was beating in her own breast. Trying to concentrate, she explained, "I mean, you've been upset at work, angry. Everybody assumes you've had business pressures...." She allowed the sentence to fade away. She had no idea why she was babbling. Maybe it was to keep her mind from wandering to the fact that Tarrant was holding her in his strong arms, peering at her with such a distracted look in his eyes.

A parody of a smile flickered across his lips. "So, my black temper has been a topic of gossip at the factory?"

"Yes. I probably shouldn't have said anything. You...you could put me down now," she tried again, sounding desperate.

Ignoring her request, he affirmed gravely, "I *have* been difficult this week." Closing his eyes for a moment, he uttered a blasphemy. When their gazes touched again, Angela was shocked by what she saw. He said nothing, but the truth was there, easy to read. She, Angela Meadows, had been the reason for his anger all week! Passions that he could no longer control burned in his dusky gaze, and she was struck by the fact that he felt the same desire she did. It was clear that he'd been fighting those feelings as strongly as she had, but it seemed they had both lost the battle. Without a word, he began to move with her toward the broad, winding staircase.

Instinctively, she knew where they were going—Tarrant's bedroom. He was going to make love to her. Against her will, she clung to him, her heart pounding madly against her rib cage. She couldn't voice a single protest, and she wasn't sure she wanted to. All the words were there, crowding her brain. *No! Stop this madness right now! Let me go! You're getting married tomorrow!* But she couldn't get the plea past her paralyzed lips. She loved Tarrant Seaton, and though she knew what he intended went wholly against both his life's plan and hers, she was helpless to intercede.

He swept into his room and lowered her lovingly to his bed. She'd seen the bedroom when she was measuring the closets, but she'd never thought she would feel the softness of his Prussian velvet spread beneath her.

"Tarrant," she managed in a whisper, "we mustn't—"

"Shh, darling," he cautioned softly, brushing her wet hair back from her face and kissing her tenderly. "Have I ever told you how beautiful you are?" he asked huskily, as he settled above her on the spread, taking her face between his hands. "That first day in the restaurant, I remember thinking how lovely you were. Then your mother walked over and told me I was going to marry you...." With a poignant smile, he shook his head at the memory. "I almost welcomed the idea—even sitting there with my fiancée." He kissed first one eyelid and then the other, murmuring, "But my life was settled, and you were suddenly just another conniving female." When his lips again grazed her mouth, he added, "I was angry with myself for being attracted to your sweet, innocent looks, knowing how deceitful you really were."

She curled her arms about his neck, protesting weakly, "But I never—"

He chuckled. It was a gentle sound that thrilled her whole body. "I don't care anymore, Angela. I don't care about motives or designs." His soft kiss sent a tingle of delight up her spine. "I just know I—"

"Tarrant?" came a woman's trill, cooling their fiery ardor.

"It's your mother," Angela whispered urgently, struggling to sit up.

"Blast it! I'd forgotten the rehearsal dinner," Tarrant muttered, standing. The emotion glistening in the dark brilliance of his eyes told her he had been deeply moved by what they'd shared. Angela felt a rush of happiness to discover that his feelings had run so much deeper than merely a calculated seduction.

Striding to the door, he opened it a crack and explained huskily, "My conference call ran longer than I'd planned. I'll meet you at the club." He slanted a somber gaze back toward Angela, and she trembled at the strength of her passion for this man. Yet even as she quivered with want, she could read regret in his eyes. He was telling her that what they had so rashly begun was now finished.

"Nonsense, dear," Delila rejoined from out in the hall. "Eden's here with me. She and I will wait for you downstairs."

Tarrant closed his eyes in frustration. "I'll be fifteen minutes."

"I noticed Angela's car out front with the hood up," Delila called again.

"It broke down. I soaked my tux trying to help her." He frowned, promising, "I'll be as fast as I can."

"How did she get home?"

Tarrant eyed the ceiling grimly, obviously hating the fact that he was being forced to lie. "I called her a taxi," he stated flatly, then closed the door.

Angela knew he'd lied to protect her reputation, and she was grateful for that. The reality of the terrible mistake they'd almost made had begun to sink in, and she shivered, more from reaction than cold. She supposed she should thank Delila and Eden for showing up when they had, but her body rebelled violently, craving Tarrant's caresses. She wanted to sob in despair at this final, ultimate rejection, but she bit her lip, trying to sustain a brave facade. She knew Tarrant wasn't marrying Eden for that "nebulous" emotion called love, so she had no argument when he'd left her huddled on his bed, in love and ashamed.

When he turned to face her, a look of sorrow was etched on his features. Could it be pity she saw there? Hurriedly, she scrambled upright, gathering what remained of her pride. He walked silently toward her, his lean body taut with frustration. Taking her hands in his, he whispered, "This is probably for the best. What I almost did was unforgivably selfish, Angela. I'm sorry."

She lowered her eyes to avoid his. "You'd better get changed," she murmured.

With a soft kiss on her cheek, he said gently, "You're cold. There's a robe in my closet. Put it on."

Without another word, he disappeared into his bathroom to shower. All Angela could do was cower there, feeling like a criminal in the night, trapped in Tarrant's bedroom with his mother and fiancée standing guard a short distance away.

By the time he got out of the shower, Angela had taken his advice and put his robe on over her clothes. She felt clammy, but less cold. When he left the bathroom, he, too, was clad in a long terry robe and was drying his hair with a towel.

She averted her gaze as he went to his closet and pulled out another tuxedo. "Angela," he said, drawing her unhappy eyes. Then he sighed and shook his head contritely. "My first instincts were right. You are a sweet, honest woman, and I'm sorry for doubting you."

She blinked in surprise, but had no time to answer, for Tarrant had returned to the bathroom to dress.

A few minutes later, he was back, slipping on another jacket, when a brief knock sounded at his door. Their eyes met, and Tarrant took Angela's hand, pulling her toward the protection of his closet. But before he could conceal her, the door swung open, and in walked Delila, chattering brightly. "Really, Tarrant, you take as long to dress as I . . ." Her words died in her throat when she saw Angela standing beside her son, clad in a robe. Color drained from the other woman's face, and quickly she closed the door, staring blankly at them both. "What is this?" she asked in a strained whisper. "Heavens, Tarrant. Tonight is your wedding rehearsal."

He pulled Angela beneath a protective arm. "Mother, this is my fault," he said quietly, "but—no thanks to me— nothing happened."

"Please, Tarrant," Angela interrupted, "don't protect me." Turning to face Delila, she offered, "Naturally, I won't come back here. I'll find someone else who can finish the remodeling job for you."

"Angela, no," Tarrant countered gently. "I insist you keep the job. Mother, I won't have you blaming her for my rashness."

Delila blinked from one of them to the other. Finally she said, "Naturally, I believe you, son. Angela, dear," she assured, "we simply won't mention this . . . this lapse."

Angela winced, feeling guilty, but she made no argument. Inwardly she vowed she wouldn't return. She couldn't bear to, no matter how gallantly Tarrant tried to make amends. At the first opportunity, she would find a replacement to finish the remodeling.

When Tarrant squeezed her shoulders, she snapped back to the present, casting him a distraught gaze. Touching her face lightly, he said, "I've become...fond of you, Angela, and I'm sorry to have caused you hurt."

She could only stare into his gleaming eyes as he continued, "I've done a lot of unpleasant things to you, but in my own defense, I must say I never lied. I'm marrying Eden tomorrow as planned, but that doesn't keep me from caring about you and wishing you every happiness." With one last bittersweet kiss, he murmured huskily, "I'd better go." He started to say something else, but seemed to think better of it; instead, he smoothed away a stray wisp of her hair. A moment later he was gone.

Angela had forgotten his mother was there until she heard the older woman clear her throat. Jerking her head up, she met Delila's pitying eyes. "I was afraid you felt this way about Tarrant," Delila lamented quietly. "I saw the way you looked at him, and I fear I know that look all too well." She sighed heavily. "I'm so sorry. For both of you."

Angela shook her head, denying the truth. "There's no reason to be, Mrs. Seaton," she lied, holding her emotions in check. "I'm fine, really." Faced with Delila's doubtful expression, Angela rushed on, "And Tarrant has already told me he doesn't believe in love."

"Yes...I know. I think I've had quite a lot to do with that philosophy of his." Moving to Angela's side, she touched her arm. "Will I see you here the day after tomorrow?"

Angela returned Delila's gaze squarely. "You know I can't come back."

Delila said nothing, looking sad.

Deciding she had little to lose at this point, Angela took Delila's hands in hers. "I've grown to care for you, Mrs. Seaton, and I want you to know..." She paused, gathering her courage to go on.

"Know what, my dear?" Delila asked.

Angela's eyes darted fitfully away, then back. "Mother told me some things about you and Noah...about Tarrant's being some sailor's child, and that you married Noah Seaton in order to give Tarrant a name." Angela hesitated, wondering about the wisdom of bringing all this up. Aware of Delila's apprehension, she hurried on, "I know we can't count on the credence of my mother's dreams, but you and I both know that she's a caring, sensitive soul. She feels deeply, and she seems able to see beneath the surface somehow."

"Yes, I sensed that about her right away, but—"

Angela interrupted, "Please, let me get this said. Mother believes Noah knew about Tarrant's being another man's son, but he loved you both anyway."

Delila's brows knit. "How could that be?" she asked, looking doubtful. "I worked so hard to keep it from him."

"I think you know he knew, Mrs. Seaton. And I think you loved him, but for some reason you've never allowed yourself to believe that. You've been too mired in guilt. Both Mother and I want you to be at peace with Noah's memory, so I hope, by saying what I have, I've helped."

Delila's eyes were glistening, but before she could speak, the chiming of a clock on Tarrant's dresser caught her attention. "Oh, it's eight o'clock. We're terribly late." Facing the tousled younger woman, Delila kissed her cheek. "Thank you, Angela. And thank Minny for me. You're both quite dear to me." Hugging Angela close, she whispered brokenly, "I'm so sorry... about everything. But I

must go. Alexander will see that you get home safely.''
With that, she hurried from the room.

The clock had struck the quarter hour before Angela
moved again. Forcing her limbs into action, she slipped
out of the robe and walked on leaden feet from Tarrant's
room. Empty inside, she trudged down the stairs. Her
mind insisted on torturing her with the fact that she was
hopelessly in love with Tarrant, and that tomorrow was his
wedding day—May twenty-third. Tears blurring her vision, she almost crashed into Alexander.

"Chauncey will escort you home, miss," he offered
quietly, his voice oddly downcast.

Unable to face him, she muttered something she hoped
sounded like a thank-you and dashed out into the drizzle
to duck into the back of one of the Seatons' limousines. It
was fortunate that both Chauncey and Alexander were
gentlemen, she mused unhappily. They would never gossip about what a fool Angela Meadows had allowed herself to be. That, at least, was something she could be
thankful for.

ANGELA HAD LEFT RICHARD to handle things in the store
while she went upstairs to have lunch. Now, an hour later,
she still hadn't eaten. The very thought of food made her
queasy. All her demented mind seemed able to do was
concentrate on the kitchen clock as the minute hand
dragged itself tediously around. One hour from now, Tarrant and Eden would be married.

She fingered the piece of bread she'd gotten out when
she thought she was going to make herself a sandwich. A
few more minutes of idle fiddling turned the slice of bread
into a plate of crumbs. Irritated with herself, she pushed
up from the table. This foolish clock-watching was doing
her no good. She might as well go back downstairs and

work. The most she could hope for was a busy day—maybe even a crisis in the store—to keep her mind off—

The ringing of the phone startled her. Without much interest, she picked up the receiver. "Hello?"

"Sweetie? Is that you?"

"Mother?" Angela sat down on a kitchen chair, worried. Minny sounded upset. "Are you okay?"

"Oh my, no! I've turned my ankle. I can't walk!"

Angela shot to her feet. "Where are you? I'll be right there." Thank heaven Chauncey had found the difficulty with her car and had delivered it to her in working order early that morning.

"Pick me up behind Sunny's Tint 'n' Dye Shoppe."

"I'll be right there." Hanging up the phone, she grabbed her car keys and dashed downstairs, hastily telling Richard where she was going.

Angela drove to the shop, convincing herself that her mother would be fine, but berating herself for wanting a crisis! She knew she shouldn't feel guilty; she hadn't caused her mother to twist her ankle. And it was becoming more and more apparent that even a crisis wouldn't get her mind off Tarrant's impending marriage.

Worse luck, the back of Sunny's Tint 'n' Dye Shoppe happened to be across the alley from the church where Tarrant and Eden were going to be married. Angela couldn't think of a worse coincidence.

Pulling her car to a screeching halt, she jumped out and ran into the shop, searching for her mother. Then, remembering Minny had asked to be met behind the store, she found the rear exit, and went in search of her injured mother.

"Mother?" she called, distraught, fearing Minny had passed out from the pain and was lying in some gutter. This alleyway, though, was quite clean and clear of refuse, except for Sunny's two trash cans and the church's Dumpster. Angela hurried over to look behind it. No Minny.

Upset and frustrated, she started back to the shop, only to come to a stumbling halt. Tarrant was standing there, resplendent in his dark gray morning coat. When he saw her, his expression grew startled. "Angela?" he asked.

She felt horrible. He would think she was spying on his wedding! "Tarrant, I—" She cut herself off when she saw Eden follow him from the church, looking like a fairy-tale queen in a flowing gown of beige lace and silk. Stunned, she watched as Eden took Tarrant's hands and kissed him fondly. The wedding must have been earlier than the paper had reported. It was clear that they were attempting to avoid reporters by sneaking out the rear entrance. Unwilling to witness their kiss, Angela turned away. How had this humiliating mistake happened? Where was her mother? What a horrible May twenty-third this was turning out to be!

Angela wanted nothing more than to run, but she could visualize her mother writhing in pain somewhere. She couldn't desert her in her time of need, no matter how dreadful this chance meeting with Tarrant and his new bride.

She scanned the alley again to avoid seeing the married couple nearby. *Mother, where are you?* she cried mentally. Maybe someone had helped her into the church. Deciding she'd better check, she forced her legs to take her in the direction of Tarrant and Eden—Mr. and Mrs. Seaton.

A taxi cruised up, and Angela stifled a sad sigh. Thank heaven they would soon be gone. A car door opened and closed. When she reached the church's back entrance, she heard the cab drive away, and stopped for a moment to regain her composure, grasping the doorjamb for support. Tarrant was gone. He and his bride were off on their honeymoon to Paris, Rome—she didn't remember where. And didn't care.

"Don't go, Angela," came a soft, deep-voiced command. Suddenly she was almost too weak to stand, for the words had been uttered by the Prince of Delights himself. How could that be? He and his wife had left.

Twisting slowly around, she was shocked to see Tarrant, alone in the alleyway.

"Tarrant?" Her voice was a disbelieving squeak. "What are you doing here?"

His expression serious, he parried with, "I might ask you the same question."

Her cheeks grew hot. "Mother hurt her ankle. I'm supposed to pick her up here."

He came toward her. Even though she stood on a step, he loomed above her, painfully handsome and powerful. His eye roving over her neat, but not new, yellow cotton dress, he repeated, "Your mother hurt her ankle—here?"

Angela grimaced helplessly. "I know it sounds crazy, but she phoned and asked me to meet her here. I really wasn't spying—"

His resonant chuckle took her off guard, so that she forgot what she had been trying to say. Leaning against the church's stone wall, he shoved his hands into his pockets, appearing casually dignified. "Nothing about you or your mother surprises me anymore. I believe you."

He looked so princely, so unobtainable, that Angela could only stare sadly. His haunting scent was working its magic, and she found herself hard-pressed to keep from touching him. She knew she had to get hold of herself. Apparently Eden had gone somewhere to change. But why, oh why, did Tarrant have to engage her in idle conversation? How could he be so insensitive to her feelings? Well, she'd be darned if she'd let him see her pain. If he insisted on a meaningless chat, that's what he would get. Straining to be polite, she asked, "So, what time's your flight?"

His gaze skimmed her controlled features. "I have a story to tell you, Angela. Do you have a few minutes?" he asked soberly.

Feigning interest in the Dumpster, she shrugged.

"First, I want to apologize about something," he began. "My mother is a good judge of people. She trusted your mother to be compassionate, just as she trusted you to be honest. I should have listened to her."

Angela wanted only to get away from his confusing presence. It was clear that, being a practiced gentleman, he was tossing her a complimentary bone, and that hurt her pride. Wishing she could disappear, she mumbled, "Whatever. Listen, I've really got to go find my mother...."

"Look at me," he ordered gently. When he had her unwilling attention, he began, "Last night, hours before dawn, Mother woke me, in tears, and told me everything. She admitted that a sailor named Lyon was my father, and that she'd tricked Noah into marrying her, then convinced him that I was his child. She told me that all these years she'd felt a gnawing guilt about it, but rationalized her deceit because her growing chocolate assets replenished the dwindling Seaton fortunes—money in exchange for an heir, so to speak.

"She could never rid herself of the guilt for her lie. That's why she'd always told me the best marriages were partnerships—not built on foolish emotions, but from honest contracts for mutual support and gain." When Tarrant took Angela's hands, she squirmed a little, hating her immediate reaction to his touch. But she couldn't bring herself to move away as he went on, "And last night, when you told her that Minny was sure Noah knew her secret and loved her anyway, it set her to thinking.''

''Thinking?'' Angela asked, her voice weak. ''About what?''

''Her marriage philosophy. She realized she *had* loved Noah—practically from the beginning—and their marriage had been a good one, not the sham her guilt had forced her to believe it was. You did her a great service by allowing her to see that.''

Something in his face changed slightly, and his eyes darkened with emotion. Angela regarded him closely. ''How are you taking all this news?'' she asked.

''As far as I'm concerned, I'm Noah's son. But it's ironic to find that my own mother used deceit to get a man to marry her. It's even stranger to learn that she did it for me.'' Sadness glistened in his eyes. ''She must have cringed every time I talked about deceitful women.''

''You didn't know,'' Angela soothed, wanting to take him into her arms, comfort him, but knowing she had no right.

''I suppose I'll have to make do with that,'' he mused. ''But we're both glad the truth is out. Mother told me she always wished she could have told Noah the truth. As it was, she used him, and because she could never forgive herself for that, she couldn't believe Noah would forgive her. And she kept her painful secret.''

''Poor Delila.'' Angela sighed.

''Yes. It was hard on her. But I have to admit one thing. Your mother's dreams may not be on track, but her heart is. She's taken a great burden from my mother's soul.''

Angela felt a small, melancholy smile lift her lips. ''Do you mean that my mother's meddling actually helped someone?''

"Yes. Thanks to Minny, Mother finally realizes Noah loved her and would have forgiven her anything." He shook his head and smiled sadly. "So, on the eve of my wedding, she decided she had to tell me that she now knows people should marry for love. She didn't want me to make a mistake because of her foolishness."

"Mistake?" Angela repeated the word without understanding.

Tarrant scanned her face, and a twinkle sparked to life in his eyes as he taunted softly, "Aren't you curious about where Eden went?"

A shiver of anxiety ran up Angela's spine at the reminder of his bride. "I assume she went to change." A forlorn note had crept into her voice, and she winced at the sound.

With an enigmatic smile, he agreed, "Yes. But there's more."

She grew very still, wondering at his odd tone. "Where did she go?"

"To Texas."

"Texas?" Angela whispered, confused.

"Did I mention Eden and I aren't married?" A thoroughly dashing grin blossomed on his lips as he watched her eyes widen in surprise.

"You're not?"

He laughed softly. "By some crazy mix-up, the church is being fumigated. During the confusion, Eden and I had a chance to talk."

Trembling, Angela listened in stunned silence as he went on, "Having had a number of hours to think about my mother's confession, I finally realized I couldn't go through with my marriage to Eden. I told her we'd been wrong to think we could be happy without passion. Without being in love. She admitted her ex-husband had called her several times, wanting a reconciliation, and she had a feeling the mistaken fumigation was an act of fate—that we'd both been given another chance to find real happiness. So Eden's gone to Texas to see him. I wish her all the best."

With a fleeting smile of recollection, he added, "I told the poor confused guests the wedding was off and that the bride had decided I would make a better friend than a husband. While reporters scurried for phones, we escaped out the back. I wanted to see Eden off—and seek out the woman I love."

Angela's throat closed with emotion. She stood there, rooted to the step, not daring even to hope.

"Angela," he began, his voice soft and husky, "I was ignorant about the subject of love until a delightfully eccentric woman entered by life and pointed out a raven-haired enchantress who had the power to show me the truth." His kiss took her by surprise, telegraphing a longing that Angela could feel all the way to her toes. Lifting his head slightly, he vowed, "Darling. I love you. Marry me. Today." He lifted her into his arms, which was a good thing for she had lost her ability to stand.

Afraid to believe her own ears, she cried, "Oh, Tarrant . . . you can't mean—"

"Of course he does, sweetie!" admonished Minny as she scampered down the steps from the church, arm in arm with an older man clad in overalls.

"Mother?" Angela gasped. "Your ankle. It's okay?"

"Why, of course it is. Hello, son," she added with a knowing grin. "I'd like you two to meet my new gentleman friend, Melvin Smedley—of Smedley's Fumigating." Her impish smile said it all. Act of fate, indeed!

Tarrant and Angela, faced with yet another sample of Minny's meddling, glanced at each other and then back at the older couple before they burst out laughing.

"Mother! You hired this man to fumigate the church?"

"Of course. You children were certainly taking your time discovering you were in love. Something had to be done!" Minny crossed her arms about her billowing frock, adding, "Besides, Melvin has a six-month easy-payment plan."

Tarrant turned to gaze at Angela, twin devils lighting his eyes. "Bless Melvin's advertising strategy," he said through a chuckle.

"Well, son, are you just going to carry my daughter around all day?" Minny inquired sternly.

He slanted her an amused glance. "What would you suggest I do with her?"

Tugging Melvin forward, she said, "Melvin's truck is right around the corner. I suggest you two go somewhere and get married. Angela, I must say, you're awfully slow-witted for a Meadows. You should have said yes by now!"

"Mother, we can't get married today." She faced Tarrant inquiringly. "Can we?"

"You have no choice, sweetie," Minny interrupted. "It's May twenty-third."

He grinned at Angela and winked. "I know a judge who owes me a favor. We'll get married today, then do it up right later." Nuzzling her ear, he whispered, "After all, our wedding date was preordained."

She hugged his neck, unable to believe Tarrant Seaton had actually proposed to her.

"Come on, you two. You can make goo-goo eyes later," Minny called. "You'll have to ride in the back of Melvin's van with the fumigating tanks. But at least the reporters won't suspect anything."

Settled among Melvin's disinfecting paraphernalia, Tarrant drew Angela into his embrace. The van lurched to a start, and she bumped her head on a metal shelf. "Ouch!" she cried, seeing an explosion of white and a burst of colorful stars. Rubbing the spot, she wondered if she was going to have these visions every time she bumped her head while in Tarrant's arms.

"Darling," he said, pulling her into his lap and scanning the spot just above her temple. "I don't think it's too bad. How do you feel?"

With a slow shake of her head, she laughed softly. "Oh, Tarrant, I'm not sure you want to know." Lifting her arms about his neck, she kissed the outrageously sexy cleft in his chin, murmuring, "But it's lucky you're having so much remodeling done in the mansion closets."

"Why?" he asked with a slow smile, revealing a dashing dimple in his cheek.

"Because, my future husband, you're going to be the father of three little girls."

"Three? Are you sure?"

With a demure lowering of her lashes, she teased, "Why don't we just wait and see?"

His chuckle filled the small space where they sat, and he kissed her deeply, drawing from her a delighted sigh.

They heard a clattering above their heads and glanced up to see Minny opening a small window that separated the cab of the vehicle from the rest of the van. "You'll have a boy first," she prophesied. "I have the power, don't forget."

When the window closed again, they smiled at each other. As Tarrant watched the woman he loved, he vowed seductively, "I have a certain power, too, my love. Would you care to know what it is?"

With his lips gently devouring hers, Angela was well aware of the answer. Content with her fate, she silently agreed that Tarrant *did* have a certain power. After all, he wasn't known as the Prince of Delights for nothing....

HARLEQUIN
Romance®

and WEDDINGS go together—
especially in June!
So don't miss next month's title in

THE BRIDAL COLLECTION

LOVE YOUR ENEMY
by Ellen James

THE BRIDE led the anti-Jarrett forces.
THE GROOM was Jarrett!
THE WEDDING? An Attraction of Opposites!

Available this month in
THE BRIDAL COLLECTION

THE MAN YOU'LL MARRY
by Debbie Macomber
Harlequin Romance (#3196)
Wherever Harlequin books are sold.

WED-2

Janet Dailey's perennially popular Americana series
continues with more exciting states!

Don't miss this romantic tour of America through
fifty favorite Harlequin Presents novels, each one set
in a different state, and researched by Janet and her
husband, Bill.

A journey of a lifetime in one cherished collection.

June titles   **#33 NORTH CAROLINA**
That Carolina Summer

#34 NORTH DAKOTA
Lord of High Lonesome

HARLEQUIN
Romance®

Coming Next Month

#3199 A CINDERELLA AFFAIR Anne Beaumont
They met one stormy day in Paris—and fell in love. Their affair was brief, yet sweet and loving. It ended when Briony realized she must return to England to marry Matthew. But how can she leave Paul for a life that will have no meaning?

#3200 WILD TEMPTATION Elizabeth Duke
Bram Wild, her new boss, has a legendary reputation as a womanizer, but Mia feels sure she's immune to his wicked charms. After all, she's happy with her dependable fiancé—and why in the world would Bram be interested in her in any case . . . ?

#3201 BRAZILIAN ENCHANTMENT Catherine George
When Kate arrives in Villa Nova to teach English, the tiny Brazilian mountain town begins to work its magic on her. The same couldn't be said of her imperious employer, Luis Vasconcelos, whose rude welcome makes Kate resolve to avoid him. But that's something that proves rather difficult.

#3202 LOVE YOUR ENEMY Ellen James
They're natural enemies. Lindy MacAllister, dedicated conservationist. She's determined to protect ''her'' colony of burrowing owls. Nick Jarrett, designer of airplanes. He's equally determined to get his new factory built, on schedule and on the selected site. When the immovable object (Lindy) meets the irresistible force (Nick)—watch out!
LOVE YOUR ENEMY is the second title in Harlequin Romance's The Bridal Collection.

#3203 RUNAWAY FROM LOVE Jessica Steele
The job offer in Thailand seems heaven-sent to Delfi. She has to get away—she's afraid she's becoming attracted to her sister's fiancé! Yet, alone in Bangkok, with Boden McLaine the only person she can turn to, Delfi wonders if she's jumped from the frying pan into the fire!

#3204 NEW LEASE ON LOVE Shannon Waverly
Nick Tanner is exactly the kind of man Chelsea wants. He's dynamic, attractive and his little daughter, Katie, is adorable. Nick even seems to be sending out the right messages . . . to the wrong woman!

OVER THE YEARS, TELEVISION HAS BROUGHT
THE LIVES AND LOVES OF MANY CHARACTERS INTO
YOUR HOMES. NOW HARLEQUIN INTRODUCES YOU
TO THE TOWN AND PEOPLE OF

One small town—twelve terrific love stories.

GREAT READING...GREAT SAVINGS...AND A FABULOUS
FREE GIFT!

Each book set in Tyler is a self-contained love story; together, the
twelve novels stitch the fabric of the community.

By collecting proofs-of-purchase found in each Tyler book, you can
receive a fabulous gift, ABSOLUTELY FREE! And use our special
Tyler coupons to save on your next TYLER book purchase.

Join us for the fourth TYLER book,
MONKEY WRENCH by Nancy Martin.

*Can elderly Rose Atkins successfully bring a new love into
granddaughter Susannah's life?*